Split Aces:

A novella by

M.L. Schepps

Advanced Reader Praise For **Split Aces**

"Part noir drama, part sci-fi thriller, and part meditative essay on the creative process, *Split Aces* is **a reading experience unlike any other.** The book is smart, playful, and wholly unexpected."
Joshua James Amberson— Author Of "Everyday Mythologies" and founder of Antiquated Future

"In *Split Aces*, M. L. Schepps has crafted a delicious noir indulgence with all the requisite tropes: down-and-out protagonist, seedy digs, drinks and drugs and a mysterious stranger. **But clever twists and a mix of introspection, language play, and science fiction take it to another level. This book marks the beginning of a promising career."**
Michael McGregor— Author of "Pure Act: The Uncommon Life of Robert Lax"

"I was hooked from the beginning of *Split Aces*. Jimmy and the world of Rawpump are captivating, and the questions the story asks left me thinking long after the final page. **A stunning exploration of our society's obsession with self-improvement wrapped up in a really great story!"**
Lauren Hobson—Founder and Editor-in-Chief of *Kithe Journal*

For Everyone Who Helped:

Pam

Maya

Mom

For all The Acknowledgements—I am deeply indebted to everyone who gave feedback, blurbed, taught, reviewed, and supported me. You all are the best.

And, especially, Molly E. Simas, editor extraordinaire, for helping make the vision of this book a reality.

CHAPTER ONE

There's a special energy you find working the blackjack grave in Rawpump; a drowsy desire that sighs with cigarette breath and insists, "you belong. You're in the right place." I'd learned to savor it as the floor drained of the daytripping Nevada tourists, leaving me with the DIGs and the DOGs, the drunks and the drifters, all the other assorted dregs—the pre-dawn losers with nowhere left to go and nothing left to do but play another round.

That night had been a quiet one, until the man showed up. I'd had a good tipper earlier in the evening, a sad-eyed divorcee who'd won her hands and left me with $20. But she was long gone by the time the man sat down. For at least an hour, I'd only been dealing to the pair of Degenerate Old Grandmas who'd camped out on my table all night. At the man's intrusion, the two biddies squawked and clucked indignantly, aghast that their carefully calibrated systems, built on a combination of odds charts and ancient wisdom, might be disrupted by the presence of a stranger.

The newcomer didn't seem to mind. "Good morning ladies," he said, in a voice with a familiar lilt that echoed brightly in my head. "Mind if I join you?" One stared blankly while the other nodded with the grace of an Empress Dowager.

"If you play smart," one DOG insisted, in a bitter schoolmarm's tone, "not an 'asshole-hits-on-seventeen' type of play. This one," she nodded at me, "he's lucky. If you play smart, you can make money."

The man turned to me and I met his gaze and, all at once, something mean and sharp swam up from deep below: an awareness of an awareness, a shadow of a thought. I knew him from somewhere, knew his face but couldn't place it. Adrenaline and recognition and confusion rushed in. I couldn't break his gaze. His eyes, something about his eyes, made me feel unmoored, like a ship that had its anchor cut and now floated, untethered and lost. As if, in his presence, there was nothing solid left to hold me in place.

Mind racing, I studied his face. The man looked younger than me, but not by much, maybe early thirties. His eyes were bright and sparkling and his face handsome. There were no bags under them, just a spray of laugh-lines instead of the scowl that was beginning to feel engraved in mine. He wore clean black jeans and a dark maroon Armani sports coat over a black T-shirt.

His posture and trim figure made me self-conscious. My stomach felt swollen and bloated—the legacy of a wolfed-down gas station burrito right before shift—and something about this guy, his presence, sent a tendril of acid up from the depths. I patted my pocket for my Tums and winced when I felt the empty wrapper. Fuck. Another acid reflux sunrise.

"You in?" I asked, looking down at the table space. My voice was steady, the casual tone giving no hint of my strange distress. The dealer face is an easy one for me to put on and, after a year on the job, it had already become second nature. The man had a small stack of chips in front of him. My eyes widened when I saw they were $50 blues instead of the expected $5 reds. If you're dropping $50 a hand on blackjack, why the fuck would you be in The Deuces Wild, a chintzy casino with cheap comps and a pack of seething DOGs all around you?

But then again, every encounter at The Deuces Wild was its own little mystery, the climax of a sad story ending in the narrative cul-de-sac that was this casino. You could go crazy trying to figure it all out, I reminded myself. Some things just weren't meant to be answered.

The man held my gaze for a moment, with both DOGs shooting impatient glances at me to deal the next hand. "I'm in," he answered, putting down the $50 chip. The women barked at one another. They were both playing the $5 minimum.

The round went quickly. Blackjack is a simple game. It's player versus dealer, both trying to get to "21" without going over. Every player at the table gets dealt two cards, face-up. Every card is worth face value except face cards—those are worth ten. And the aces, well, they're special. They can be either a one or an eleven, depending on the whim of the player and the value of the deal.

The dealer has no actual choices: they have to adhere to prescribed behaviors, based on the value of their cards. It's these rigid rules of dealer conduct that make the game so appealing to the DOG contingents. A smart player who simply follows the instructions of a blackjack odds chart—the little laminated cards that literally tell a player what to do and when to do it in every single possible situation—has close to a fifty percent chance of a win over the dealer. You won't get odds like that anywhere else in a casino.

I dealt the man a 14 and the two DOGs a 15 and an 18. Those were all good hands. I had a six showing and a king hid. It was the man's turn. He was hesitating.

"The dealer shows six," the talkative DOG emphasized. "That means you stand. Don't mess us up." The other nodded her head with imperious ferocity.

This kind of bold insistence is the hallmark of a DOG and their primary difference with a DIG. Your basic Degenerate Idiot Gambler? They don't come to win, not really. They come to self-destruct in a grand and flashy manner. What they want is to lose it all, to feel the fall. They may not know it but what they're doing is just a slow, protracted suicide.

DOGs are different. They want to play. It's all they want to do, to ride that thin line between win and loss—to run that razor's edge as long as they can. They memorize the odds charts, scorn the fools at the slots ("no player edge!"), and camp out at the tables for a dozen hours at a stretch, riding the ebbs and the flows. By following all the advantage charts, they break even more often than not. They don't win big but they don't lose big.

The one thing they hate the most are the DIGs.

When a pack of DOGs is working a table, they're merciless. They all know just what to do according to the odds, betting slow and steady and riding the rhythm. But if a DIG sits down and fucks up the works? Hits when he's not supposed to and disturbs the system? Then that's it. A whole evening of careful calibration is destroyed.

So when the stranger in the red sport coat made the "hit me" motion on a '14' the reaction was instant. "NO!!" shouted the talkative DOG, while the other made an outraged grimace. The charts could not be clearer: when the dealer has a six and you've got 14, you hold.

The man gave them both a smile. I saw languid confidence wafting from him like gas fumes, making the room feel woozy with his assurance. He appeared to be that type of man, the sort who always knows just what to say and do and then just goes ahead and does it.

"Pardon my play ladies, I'm feeling lucky," he drawled.

That did nothing to mollify the angry DOGs. "Lucky" was a lie. DOGs have systems.

I dealt the man a seven and triggered a chorus of groans. "Twenty-one," I said, "big winner."

Neither woman took a card. I turned mine over and showed 16. The dealer always has to hit on 16. I drew a four and ended up with twenty. I passed the man his chips and took the women's, avoiding their eyes, which bulged apoplectically in their fury. If the man had followed their advice—their system—and did what the odds said to do, he'd have stayed on 14. The women would have stayed as well. I would have been forced, as dealer, to draw his seven and bust, meaning everyone else at the table would have won.

The women stood indignantly, gathered their chips and left the table without another word—and certainly without a tip. These two had been my companions throughout this entire shift, five long hours with them at this table, throughout the highs and the lows. And, at the end, they left me with nothing, not even a $5 chip. It was a nice little "fuck you," to go alongside the minimum wage pay from the Deuces. I gave a bitter laugh. At least there was some satisfaction in being right. It's true what they say: old DOGs don't surprise you by learning new tricks.

Just the two of us remained, me and this strangely familiar stranger.

"Nice play," I said. It wasn't. Hunches and lucky feelings weren't real. What was real were the odds and the long view and the house edge. Given enough time and enough struggle, you'll lose and the house will win. It's always that way.

"Thank you," he responded. I waited for him to put down his next bet. He didn't. He just stared at me, unabashed and rude.

My uneasy feeling grew. The dealer's mask slipped, and I started to chatter.

"There's no table service now," I said. "The cocktail girls don't work the graveyard. There'll be breakfast service in about an hour, though. Buffet of Enchantment, they call it. Even has an omelette station. Bottomless mimosas. Not bad, really."

I knew I was rambling but couldn't help it. Something about this man's quiet confidence left me feeling uncertain and unnerved. He seemed so familiar, yet I was sure we'd never met. Recognition crouched on the edges of my awareness and a flush of cold sweat under my arms made me cautious. Did I know him? Did he know me?

There were hard years, drinking years, that I could barely remember. Whole years that I knew were bad but didn't know how. The drinking and drugs had cast so much of my past in a dim light, a darkness at which my memory probed and squinted and came up blank. The man could be an old friend from those bad days. He could be an enemy. He could even be a stranger, and my dissociation the result of fried synapses. I just didn't know.

I felt adrift again, unmoored from the safe harbors of the day-to-day, tugged blindly by deep currents.

"Buffet of Enchantment? Huh." The man was impassive, his gaze shifting slowly from my face to my uniform. I felt my cheeks flush as he took in the too-tight fit around my gut and the faded but still present guacamole stain over my heart.

"Yes sir. Downright enchanting. Like Merlin and Gandalf were working the waffle-makers," I said, smiling, surprising myself. You weren't supposed to banter like this with the guests. You took their bets, laughed at their dumb jokes and stayed professional.

His face broke into a grin, a winning one that made me feel good in response. "Hmm, I think I may be more in the mood for something slightly more practical. Something serious," he mused. "Like pensive pancakes."

"Or wistful waffles," I answered, making us both laugh.

"Goes well with somber smoothies," the man responded.

"Just the thing to wash down those biscuits and grave."

"Biscuits and grave," he repeated with a smile. "I like that." He thrust out his hand. "JD," he said.

"I'm Jimmy," I replied. "How do you do?"

As soon as I shook his hand, I felt the oppressive gaze of Eduardo the pit-boss staring at me from across the room. Asshole. I saw him start to lumber over from the mini-bac.

"I do quite well Jimmy. Do you?" JD said. I stared at him. He stared back. There was something in those eyes, that face. There was a distant memory, a knowledge that stalked my consciousness ready to ambush. I just couldn't see it.

"Your bet, sir," I said professionally, right as Eduardo heeled up, looming over my shoulder. JD gave the pit boss a dismissive look and stood, but not before putting down five blue $50 chips.

"Think I'm played out," he said. "But you've earned that tip, Jimmy." JD looked up at Eduardo, who struggled between confusion and the requisite glad-handing and schmoozing that is integral to the casino business. Finally, he seemed to settle on both, giving JD a big smile with suspicious eyes.

"I hope it was a good morning, sir. Did Jimmy here tell you about our Buffet of Enchantment?" Eduardo asked, looking at the two of us with a glare.

"Sounds magical," JD said. "A frittata fantasia perhaps, old sport?"

I blinked, my memories falling into place. He'd said "old sport," a phrase with a familiar ring to it. Suddenly, I knew where I knew him from. Or, at least, I knew what he reminded me of.

The man spoke with the exact same tone of detached irony—full of verbal curlicues, alliteration and puns—as Brewster Bradley, my high school English instructor from Reynolds Academy. JD's affectations, his accent, his tone, our banter over breakfast foods: it was boarding school days all over again. That was the familiarity. With him, that tone still came across as charming and insouciant. On me, it had moldered into bitter sarcasm.

He was clearly another Reynolds man—the "old sport" made me certain. That particular phrase was one Brewster Bradley had said constantly. When we finally read *The Great Gatsby*, it became a part of the whole class's vocabulary.

I felt it like an itch between my eyes, the frustration of not fully remembering this man. I silently cursed all the befogged and drink-filled years that stood between now and then, forming an impenetrable wall with bricks made of black-outs and time, still keeping me from the truth.

"I think I'll pass on the buffet. For today at least," JD continued. He looked away from Eduardo and right back at me. "Are you working tomorrow?"

I nodded. "Same shift."

"Different day," responded JD.

Eduardo cleared his throat. "Will you be wanting a private table, sir?" he asked. "That can be arranged if you're in the mood. We can set you up quite nicely, with some of our senior dealers? Drink service?"

"I just want Jimmy," JD replied, giving me an exaggerated wink. "Until tomorrow."

And off he walked.

The rest of the shift passed quickly. Eduardo gave me shit about improper fraternization. The DOGs slunk back and spent the rest of the time talking about "that asshole" hitting on 14. The whole time I felt detached and strange, barely thinking about what I was doing while I obsessed over the unreliability of memory. All the long and bitter years since high school made a mental gap, a yawning chasm which I kept trying desperately to bridge. The man was from Reynolds Academy at least, I was certain.

Wasn't I?

CHAPTER TWO

There are no clocks in a 24 hour casino. No windows. We don't want our guests to consider the passage of time. We just want them there until their money is gone. But you learn to pick up wayposts, certain signs, when you work there long enough. The ceremonial Changing of the DOGs was mine, when the bedraggled night shift gave way to the chipper cohorts piling out of their chartered buses and retirement community vans with fresh bouffants and bulging wallets.

I walked into the parking lot just as the sun broke through with a harsh and condemning gaze. Sunrises are quick and mean in the desert —they don't allow for any illusions. It's just you and that boundless, burning eye. My stomach flamed with indigestion, acid reflux shredding my throat, as the desert cast off its night-cold and started to bake.

The long walk back to my car gave me time to think. I always parked as far as I could from the entrance in the employee lot. There was a time when, grasped by one of my periodic fevers of self-improvement, I told myself it was to "get my steps in," feeling smug about making the righteous kind of choice which, when piled on with other good decisions, can make for a healthy lifestyle. That didn't last. Now I kept up the habit out of shame, as the mess in my backseat increased in lockstep with my diminished urge to better myself. Instead of trying to be healthier, I just didn't want my co-workers to witness the sea of wrappers and trash that had filled my backseat, and was now slow-motion surging into the front in a great frothy wave of defeat, ennui, and grease.

There was a half-eaten gas station pastry waiting for me on my seat. It had been bad fresh and was worse stale, but I didn't care. It was still sugar and carbohydrates, a momentary pleasure. It left more acid in its wake, but still. There was that moment.

I wilted during the drive home, the sun as unmerciful as the wide unblinking stare of God.

Rawpump is a funny little town, halfway between Death Valley and Las Vegas. There are only a few reasons to live in Rawpump: military, desert recreation, hard drugs, and desperation. The city and its sprawl form an archipelago of shitty casinos, truck stops, army wives, bargain brothels, and Mormons in a vast sea of desert. If you're not here for the desert or the army or the crank, you're here because you ended up here. You had nowhere else to go.

I lived in an old motel converted into extended stay. When I'd first seen the Gem-And-I Inn, I'd fallen in love with the classic 1950s styling, the faded retro mid-century kitsch that promised a life of inspiration and adventure à la Kerouac or Kesey's Merry Pranksters. It was the kind of place a writer should live, a place with a thousand stories just waiting to be told.

In the limpid light of early morning, the motor court just looked tired, whatever stories it held as sun-bleached and dusty as the paint. I pulled into the parking space in front of my unit, empty as usual. There weren't a lot of permanent residents at the Gem-And-I: a few other casino workers, some undocumenteds hot-sheeting six-to-a-room, and the quiet opiate addicts who showed up every month when their disability checks came, returning faithfully like Capistrano's nodding-off swallows. My neighbors.

And me.

Still, it wasn't bad. It was cheap and clean and the Judsons—a family of a dozen from Provo who owned it—ran a reasonably tight ship. Hookers and drug dealers got turned out quick, and they kept a close watch for tweakers.

I was fortunate that I liked the Judsons and the Judsons liked me. The whole family had taken me on as a project, trying to fix my life with their determined Latter Day sincerity. Pa Judson (I'd long ago forgotten his real first name) was already out front in the motor court, sweeping the sidewalks with a gaggle of his buck-toothed and winsome kids all helping out. Three of the older ones were wearing basketball uniforms and jogging laps around the property.

"Good morning, Jim! Say hello to Mr. Dougherty, kids!" Pa Judson bellowed.

"Hello Mr. Dougherty!" sang a chorus of tiny towheaded Mormons, looking up from their chores.

"Good evening kids," I said, making them laugh. The tired jokes I'd make about the night-shift still made those kids smile.

"Cezoram, Jakkalynn—I need to speak with Mr. Dougherty a moment. Make sure the walks get clean, and make sure your siblings help!" Pa set his little workers to happy tasks before continuing with, "Bill, Vackenzie, Gurt: I want to see twelve more laps before breakfast!"

Once the swarm of Mormons was released to buzz about in contented productivity, Pa turned to me. "Given any more thought to that invite, Jim?"

I hadn't. Pa and Ma Judson had decided I needed to be saved from the life of unmarried secular sin and were cheerfully determined to be the ones to rescue me. Pa had a friend from church who worked in oil and gas out in Mohave and needed dependable and intelligent workers. Pa and Ma were always extending invites to come to dinner with that friend and/or that buxom LDS widow they were always going on about. It was a transparent trap. Take the job, date the widow. Convert. Push out a flock of Mormons of my own and settle into the long, slow entropy of aging.

Sometimes though, when the days felt as endless as my empty nights, I admit I was tempted.

I shook my head at Pa. "Sorry Mr. Judson, it does sound appealing. God knows I miss a good woman's cooking, and Mrs. Judson is as good as they come." I loved laying on the corn with the Judsons. They never seemed to pick up the sarcasm. "But boy golly, I reckon I'll be plum pooped come Friday. I'm working on a new story, you know."

Pa had all the guardedness of a golden retriever, his emotions writ large on his wide and sunburnt face. It fell when I declined dinner, and perked right back up when I mentioned the story. He was always curious about my writing.

"Oh, that is exciting, Jim! I can't wait to read it. I'll let you get to it, huh? And think about that invite, will you? Hank would love to meet you. He's always telling me about the knuckleheads he has to hire on. Good money in oil and gas, you know! Plenty of room for advancement. And Beverly Anderson, well her little one is having some trouble with his reading and writing. Ever since her husband got called up to the Lord, she's been struggling. Ma is always after getting me to introduce you two." He gave me an exaggerated wink. "She's a determined and industrious woman, you know."

"I do know, Mr. Judson. I know very well. And thank you again for the invitation, I'm sure one of these days I'll be able to take you up on it. Now you have a good day, I've got to get to work!" I turned back to my room and opened the door, deflating all at once from the false bonhomie that dealing with the Judsons entailed.

A leering face appeared in front of me, lurching from the darkness. I jumped back, past the threshold, my heart racing—before the reality of it made me laugh. I had been surprised by my own reflection, the unfamiliar winner's smile appearing in the mirror like an interloper.

 Like a thief.

I shut the door behind me, flicking on the lights. Something about my reflection seemed different. I felt different. I gave myself a wink.

Even though my chest heaved with acid, I was hungry. But I was tired from the shift and from matching the Judson perk. The thought of walking to the fridge and making a decent breakfast exhausted me. I considered turning right around and getting something hot from a diner, or even going to McDonald's for some McDPs.

I stopped short. A McDP? I hadn't thought of one of those in decades. It was what we used to call our special breakfast sandwiches when I was back at Reynolds Academy: a "Mc-Double-Penetration," which consisted of two McMuffins (one bacon, one sausage) stacked together with a hashbrown, using ketchup and honey as the mortar. I could almost taste it.

Nothing brings back memories like smell. Sometimes even remembering a scent can trigger a memory. The ghostly whiff of a McDP pushed me into the past.

I am fifteen, walking with some of my friends into Bradley's classroom. It's a glorious Clinton-era spring, one that smells of blooming linden trees and breakfast meats and an absence of 9/11.

We're late but don't care. The six of us in the Advanced English Workshop saunter in with adolescent swagger and a greasy bag. Bradley sees us, cocks an eyebrow, ostentatiously checks his watch.

And there I am, as cool as can be, offering him a McDP in penance for the tardiness.

"What, pray tell, might this 'McDP' be, Jimmy? I don't recall ever seeing such a concoction on the menu," he asks, with that arch Bostonian tone.

"A McDelicious Pastry, sir," I answer, sparking off a round of laughter from the rest. (God, I was sharp.)

"Hmmm," Bradley responds. "A McDubious Proposition, no doubt."

"No sir, McDefinite Pleasure."

"Well, at the very least, old sport, it seems to have come with a McDuplicitous Pupil," he says with a grin.

Ah, those Reynolds days. They seemed like the prelude of a life just like that, full of witty banter and quick jokes, intellectual games.

While Bradley came to mind with vivid detail, my classmates were indistinct, their faces fuzzy and unfocused. I could see them as a chorus—laughing at my jokes, engaged in pranks, bantering in class—but the specifics are lost. That's the problem with being a class clown: you remember them laughing but never their names. They're your audience, not your peers. It was easy to see a *them*, but much harder to see a *who*. I didn't remember a single surname. Just a few first names with indistinct faces (an Andrew, a Kevin, a Charlie), but any further and I hit that hard wall of forgetting.

Part of it was the drinking years, sure. They'd done a number on my long-term memory. But mostly I'd never been all that concerned about my classmates. They were there to laugh at my jokes, swell a scene or two, but that was it.

I thought again of JD, this unknown reappearing from those years.

If I had been the sort of sentimental person who kept yearbooks, I could figure JD out, look at pictures and get a real name, which might spark some recognition. And if I'd been the kind of mush-brained sap who used Facebook, I could do the same. But I wasn't either. I'd spent too much time moving forward to worry about looking back—too many years living hard to be thinking soft.

It made me angry, this frustrated remembrance. There was something so obvious about him, staring me right in my face. But that knowledge, that lost memory, just wouldn't come. I was almost certain JD had to be from Reynolds, and I knew he clearly wanted to talk to me, so much so he'd gone to the trouble of tracking me down and showing up at the Deuce's Wild in Rawpump.

I wasn't that surprised, to tell the truth. I'd made a hell of an impression at Reynolds Academy before I got kicked out. I was clever, funny, even had some stories published that won student awards. And once, with Bradley's encouragement, I'd published something in a respectable college lit journal. Sure, I could understand why someone from back then wanted to talk to me. I just couldn't figure out why he was being so fucking coy.

♠♥♣♦

The dark box that was my apartment was blackout-curtain black and swamp-cooler cold, weighted with the feral yeast of spilled beer and stale pizza. There wasn't much to see. I've always been a minimalist. There was a small television where I could watch PBS. Next to that was the small bookcase holding the good hardcovers and a couple worn first editions with pride of place upon the shelves, alongside the stack of paperback thrillers (admittedly lurid and trite but hell, we've all got needs). There was the dining table heaped, as always, with wrappers and empties. And then there was my small walnut writing desk, with the notebook, shoebox, and pens in immaculate isolation, waiting for a purpose. By the unmade bed stood a towering mound of unwashed clothes next to an ever-shrinking pile of clean ones.

It was a bachelor's home, a writer's home. Sure, it was a little stark and untidy, but then again, so was I.

The Moleskine on the desk looked at me in blank disappointment. I felt the same shot of guilt I always did when I saw those empty pages, the ones that had been waiting for me to fill them for over a year. Here was what I'd been working on for so long: a whole lot of nothing.

I had the same reflexive thoughts I always had when I stared plainly at that absence. There was the first voice, the practical one, which told me it would be easy to write something, anything. Even just a scrap of memory or a limerick. Anything. I just had to start. Everything would happen after that first step.

But then there was the second voice, the louder one, that reminded me that even though it was easy to write, not writing was even easier. All I had to do was nothing. And I was very good at doing nothing. I had a lot of practice.

The first voice reminded me of the journey I'd taken to get here, to this motel and the misery of the unwritten page. All the years I'd spent "generating material" while dealing coke, then the years after that, working barista pumps in Los Angeles, thinking of those screenplays I'd write someday, jotting down plot ideas or scraps of dialogue onto index cards. It had been good work, with plenty of time to daydream.

But the moment never came, the moment I knew was still ahead. The one where I could, at last, become the me I was always meant to be: the writer. All I needed to do was wait until the conditions were just right. I thought of myself like a kettle on a stove. The water was my talent, the fire was my experiences. And when it all came together, I'd sing.

I respected the artistic process too much to strip it down to bare mechanics. I knew the power of the moment and of true inspiration. Everything inside of me, all these stories and scripts and ideas, would flow out unimpeded. When the moment was right.

It took me years in Los Angeles to realize that the moment wouldn't arrive so long as I lived there. After Marcia got hired to work on that sitcom, I had to leave. She was a sweet kid, right out of a small town when she started working with me at the Double Shot. Marcia was a writer too, and a good one. Real talent. We exchanged stories once. I still had the copy of mine she'd marked up with a red pen. It was only an opening couple of pages, but her insights were clear and well-observed. She was a skilled girl who used to do improv and open mics. I'd always meant to go see her perform. Never did though.

She ended up quitting the coffee shop to take an unpaid internship at some improv theatre, and had been gone a few months when word came back she'd gotten a break. Marcia had written a spec script good enough to get her staffed in a writing room. I'm talking network, WGA, a rep from CAA. The works. She'd made it.

After that I realized how phony Los Angeles was, how obsessed with youth and glib ephemera. It wasn't me. My soul had grown flabby with all the Hollywood dross. I needed to get out of there. I needed to tell true stories. I needed to live one.

I'd come to Rawpump because I'd imagined the desert as a chance to do just that, somewhere sere and pure and clean with wide Edward Abbey horizons and Hunter S. Thompson nights, a place where I could remember who I really was, refine the vital alloy of my soul, and make my moment come at last. I had a vision of easy work, desert dawns, Mojave mindset. Telling stories that had to be told.

But a year of this life had left me with nothing but blank pages and chronic acid reflux. I was sleeping too much, 10 to 12 sweaty hours at a stretch. I'd wake up and nurse beers while watching shit cable or reading trash thrillers, then walk over to the mini-mall for dinner. I'd driven out to the true desert only once and never made it past the visitor's center.

Every morning, after my shift, I'd have this same argument with myself, the two voices warring in their clear and distinct tones. The one that wanted me to work told me plainly: "You've got the time now, go write something. All you need to do is start."

"There'll be time tomorrow," the other voice responded. "Art is alchemy, it can't be stripped down to a science. The muse must speak and you must be ready to listen. Be patient. It will come—and it will be perfect."

The second voice seemed reasonable, but I recognized the wheedling tone, that one always urging the easy way. The one telling me to just keep waiting. However, it was an easy voice to listen to, compared to the harsh surety that told me that all I really needed to do was start.

And one of these days I would, I would. It wouldn't be today though.

I ate Frosted Flakes from a dirty salad bowl. I stripped down to my underwear and scrubbed at the guacamole stain on my work jacket. After a few minutes of this, I really was ready for bed, the tangled sweat-yellow sheets beckoning irresistibly. I turned the AC up to maximum, double-checked the locked door, and dreamt of wayward boats adrift on ink-black seas.

CHAPTER THREE

Eduardo made trouble for me at work. He'd reported the $250 tip I'd received up to security. No one ever tips like that at the Rawpump Deuces, unless they're a DIG going terminal with their self-destruction. Someone like this JD—who played only a single hand and then won, tipped me more than he gained, asked about my next shift and then left—raised more red flags than a Bolshevik.

Security drilled me for twenty minutes before sending me back to the tables, asking the same questions over and over as to whether or not I knew the man who'd tipped me so well. I told them I didn't and just kept repeating it. Eventually mollified, they reassigned me for the night and put me on the Big Wheel.

There's nothing simpler or stupider than the Big Wheel, which is literally a large wheel that you spin. It's got the lowest player edge in the casino and is scorned by the DOGs that make up the majority of the night action. It was right at the entrance though, and always made a good impression. I kept busy with tadpoles: community-college frat guys, single-mom bachelorette parties, middle-aged business cronies on their way back from the cheap brothels. The people who weren't really there to gamble, just to pass the time and have a little fun. No one stays at the Big Wheel. They give it a spin and move on.

The shift went quick and my mind wandered, looping around and around with thoughts of Reynolds Academy, of paths not taken, of books unwritten. I'd woken up sweaty and bedraggled and felt restless. Those dreams of drifting ships, lost in the vastness of the black, had been vivid. You didn't have to be a Freudian or an asshole with an MFA to get the symbolism. My life lacked roots and direction, nothing holding me in place and nowhere to head. I was lost and well on my way to that terminal destination of *drifter*.

The drifter is every bit as endemic to a shit-casino as the DIGs and DOGs. They're the men (always men) who sidle up, out of the corner of your eye, but never introduce themselves. The men who slink in smoke-filled corners and nurse cheap beers and don't even bother to sexually harass the waitresses. The men who've been running for so long that they forgot whether they were running towards something or away from it and then—when their red-hot engine fueled on testosterone and desperation finally stalled—ended up just drifting. From town to town, from job to job, from life to life.

I never wanted that fate but now, facing my north-30s, I felt its riptide tug. I could sense the distant tang of the true freedom which came from simply giving up. How would it feel to release all that tension, the constant droning din which stemmed from my awareness I was on the wrong path, my destination as far away as ever?

It would be easy to do, to feel myself buoyed by circumstance. To give up on the dreams and aspirations which had defined me for so long. To just be: paycheck to paycheck, six-pack to six-pack, decade to decade.

The life of a drifter was the flipside to those Judson visions of a dutiful wife and a career. It was something I could fall into, so easy. All I had to do was let go of those writer dreams which had kept me swinging above that abyss for so long. All I had to do was fall.

I was well on my way there. I knew it in my bones. I'd spent the prime of my twenties as an unsettled lowlife, a frat-house drug dealer, couchsurfing the dorms at UCLA, USC and all the rest. I was good at wearing the mask of the dealer, befriending the people I needed to befriend and making sure I could always be found when wanted and absent when not. But I wasn't good at the business angle. I dealt drugs initially just as a way to experience the *milieu* of it all; a witness to the authenticity of those wild college years for the purpose of "generating material" and "paying my dues." By the end, I was dealing just to support my own habit, the eightballs getting skinnier and skinnier until one day a couple pissed-off Kappa Sigmas gave me the two-fisted wakeup call I'd needed.

And it was a rough awakening. I was getting older, had no resume beyond "campus drug dealer," and nothing to show for those years beyond recurrent chlamydia, an addiction to cocaine, and the knowledge I could put on a good face if I needed—a bantering mask which made commerce easy. With that skill in hand, I resolved to get clean(ish), stop the coke, and get a day job.

I became a barista, a dealer in legal stimulants, and spent my late 20s and early 30s trying to be Bukowski, trading a willingness to indulge in the hard stuff for an affected cynicism built on the fact of those past indulgences. I haunted the Los Angeles dive bars, chasing the liminal beauty only found in a cheap day-drunk afternoon.

It was all still in the service of writing. I knew I had the talent, had known since I'd received the high school validation of being called a gifted student. But I also knew that talent was only part of the story, I knew I'd always lacked the purpose, the raw fuel to make my engine burn hot. I'd been stoking my engine for years now, ready for my someday.

But, with the hard drop-off of 40 looming larger and larger, I was starting to recognize there were fewer and fewer "somedays" ahead. There I was, dealing cards instead of cocaine or coffee, but it wasn't all that different. I hadn't made much progress. I was still the masked middleman, giving the addicts what they needed with a big fake smile. I was running in place: spinning my wheels, spinning the Big Wheel.

There was something deeply funny about my plight, a middle-aged man in dirty uniform standing in place by a wheel-of-fortune, waiting anxiously for someone from his past to approach and take a chance, to spin the wheel.

But that someone never did.

The darkness passed into dawn. The night DOGs gathered their payout vouchers and nodded vacantly to the day shift piling out of the chartered vans with the names of cheap retirement homes written on their sides. I clocked out, gathered my shit and went out to the parking lot.

And there he was, clean and well-rested, leaning casually on the hood of my car.

CHAPTER FOUR

JD looked more professional this time, in a dark golden-yellow blazer and matching pants worn over another black t-shirt. His face, his figure, his bearing… it was all so familiar. I was still lost, but the need to place him felt more urgent than ever. I knew the where, but was missing the *who* and the *how*. Once I had those, I could go to the *why*. If I had to let this guy lead the dance for a while, play along with him to get what I wanted? That was fine. I had plenty of practice.

"Howdy," he said, as I approached. I felt a flash of anger at his presumptuous lean upon my car, chased with shame that he should see the state of my backseat with all its detritus. The shame didn't last. It rarely did these days.

"Howdy yourself," I answered. "Not feeling lucky?"

He made a show of pinching an arm. "Feeling something, at least." It was a tired joke that still elicited a tired smile. "But seriously, I don't have much time today. I've got places I need to be, and soon. We should talk."

I felt my mask slip on, the bantering one. The one that gives a big laugh at your jokes and sets up your next punchline. It was clear that whatever the punchline was, JD's joke was an elaborate one.

"Hungry?" I asked. "Remember: 'When you've got that Thick Trouble and Consternation,'" I started, in a sing-song falsetto.

"Then Mister, you need a McDouble-Penetration!" he sang with a big smile, finishing the rhyme. My smile back was a genuine one. It was amazing how the years fell away, how much more true and vital those adolescent thoughts and memories were than the slow, heavy webs of the now.

I pointed to the McDonald's across the lot. "Let's go then, old sport."

We walked in silence across the wide expanse. By the time we got there my blood sugar was low, the acid-reflux was high, and I was back to nursing a real resentment at the elaborateness of this whole charade, this obscure practical joke which centered me as the subject. If you wanted to see an old school friend, you didn't ambush them. I reminded myself to keep playing it cool as my sudden anger warred with curiosity.

Inside it was like every sunbleached, fly-spotted, fast-food shit-shack, with the fixtures out of date and mildew in the corners. A herd of churchgoers swayed, sated with their greasy feed bags, while truckers sat solo with their morning Cokes and sunrise cheeseburgers, lost in grimy clouds of amphetamine sweat and loneliness.

"You're buying," I said, as the line of day laborers and morning-shifters moved forward.

"My pleasure," he said, before we lapsed back into silence. Our turn came. The cashier was young, pockmarked and eye-bagged, her eyebrows tattooed into permanent surprise.

"Good morning and welcome to McDonald's. May I take your order?" she asked, in a tired monotone.

"You certainly may, my dear!" JD boomed, with exaggerated good humor and a crisp mid-Atlantic affectation. "My friend and I require two sausage McMuffins, two bacon McMuffins, a dozen shucked Kumamoto on ice with mignonette, two coffee, clam chowder—"

"Manhattan clam chowder," I interrupted, "with plenty of tomato."

"Of course, goes without saying, doesn't it? We'll take a tureen of the Manhattan clam chowder." JD paused and squinted before continuing. "A full tureen, mind you, not a Scotsman's pour. And I'll also need a chateaubriand with a proper béarnaise, and, yes… let's get two sides of hash browns. Anything else?" He looked at me.

"Don't forget the roast ortolan," I said, in a voice that matched his. "They're in season." God, I couldn't help myself. I'll say this for JD, he made me laugh. Stupid shit like this still cracked me up, just like in high school.

It didn't amuse the counter girl. She just nodded, barely indulgent. "Uh uh," she said. "We got the McMuffins and what else?"

With our trays in hand, we sat down in a sticky booth and assembled our McDPs, our bodies acting in the unison of decades-old muscle memory. It was a procedure that had become every bit as ritualized and inviolate as that of a kosher or halal kitchen over the course of high school. You slather the bottom of the bacon McMuffin with ketchup (half packet) and honey (full pack). With the hashbrowns in between, you slam it on top of the sausage McMuffin while saying "Bacon wins! Fatality!" in the voice of the *Mortal Kombat* announcer.

The movements, the smell, that moment, all brought me back to Reynolds again, by the shores of Lake Winnipesaukee in the gloaming of a New England spring. I'd been young, a whole life ahead, a belly full of ambrosial cheeses and processed meats, and the metabolism to burn it all away. A whole life in front of me, limitless potential and the knowledge it would end up alright.

And now look at me. Time won. Fatality.

The words trailed off, and we were again two middle-aged men sitting in a dawn McDonald's, eating breakfast sandwiches named for pornography. They tasted like shit, my memory's echo far superior to this gummy reality. This wasn't funny. None of it was. I'd had enough: enough of this blank asshole with his cloying familiarity, enough of the McMuffins. Enough.

"So what do you do?" JD asked me, having put his sandwich down after only an exploratory bite.

"I'm a casino dealer. Obviously."

"Is the money good?"

"It's shit."

"The money?"

"What you're full of," I replied. I was tired of this game, the McDP squatting in my stomach like a toad. The mask came off. I was done playing it cool. It was cards on the table time. "You're from Reynolds Academy, right? You looked me up online, tracked me down, and here you are."

He gave me a slow nod. "I went to Reynolds. I'm not from there."

"Yeah, well. Whatever. I clearly made an impression on you. I'm not surprised. But you know what kind of impression you made on me? What I remember about you, JD? Not a goddamn thing. You're a blank to me." He just stared. "And now you show up, after 20 years of what, obsession? Jealousy? Lust? You show up to my place of employment and play dumb. Be a big shot with a tip. Two hundred and fucking fifty dollars?" I pulled out my wallet, with the five crisp fifties I'd received the night before. "Fuck you and fuck your money." I tore the wad in half and threw it down. My face felt hot and flushed, but I was good. Righteous.

JD just sat there, calm and collected. He glanced at the money, dismissed it, then gave a slow and deliberate pan around the room, a half-amused smile on his face. My indignation faded and I became aware of the hushed voices from the other patrons, the stifled giggles from the kids. My outburst had drawn a lot of attention. The heat on my face began to feel stifling.

JD gave a theatrical shrug, then pulled out an iPhone, unlocked it with his thumb, and checked the time. He put the phone back in his pocket and started to speak. "There's two guys right out of college," he drawled. "And they start a drywall business. Just a small time thing. It's the nineties, you know? They're slackers. Happy to spend their days smoking weed and drinking beer, listening to Soundgarden. And they get a job at some rinky-dink place, installing drywall in a new office. And wouldn't you know it? The new company can't make payroll that month. But this company makes them an offer: either settle for $500 now or get paid the full balance in stock options. So the first guy takes the stock offer while the other one thinks they're getting played. The second guy gets paid $250 and that's it, he goes home laughing at the credulity of his partner."

My jaw was hanging open and my blood pounded in my veins. I knew what JD was going to say next but didn't want to hear it.

"Anyway," JD continued, "the company turns out to be Google. The partner who took the stock ends up with a few million dollars when it goes public, parleys that into a couple other dumb start-up bets that get lucky. Fifteen years later and he's a billionaire, while the other guy's still working drywall. So the other guy starts to plan a heist. He's going to rob his best friend."

My throat was dry. "That's *Average Dads*," I hissed. "That's my fucking script."

"They went ahead and changed it to *Silicon Daddy*, but yeah, that's your fucking script."

Fury and rage and bafflement, a black-red haze blotting out the corner of my eyes. This cocksucker had stolen my script.

And then, with a lurch, my righteous indignation sunk away, leaving a vast void of uncertainty. What script? *Average Dads* was an idea, a few scrawled sentences on an index card sitting in a shoebox. It was a good idea, sure, one I'd worked over a few times in my head. *Average Dads* was going to be a real parable about the bitter futility of the American dream, one where dumb luck meant a lot more than hard work. The script was going to be biting, funny, and mordant—I saw it again and again. I'd play out a few scenes, consider some dialogue. It felt real.

But it was all unwritten. Just a few lines on a notecard and whatever was in my mind.

JD was standing and I wanted to hit him, to just wipe the smirk off his face. I'd never been a good fighter, always been better at being hit than hitting, but at that moment I could kill. "What the fuck—" I started.

"I've got answers. I do." JD sounded rushed. "But I've got to go right now. Time got away from me and I can't stay. But I promise you this: I'm not going to fuck you around, Jim. I'm not here to do that. I'm here to help you. I'm here to do things for you no one ever has. I'm going to change your life, my man. I'm going to change your life."

"Fuck you and fuck your assurances. Get out of my sight, asshole," I snarled. I wasn't going to give him the satisfaction. I didn't care what sick shit, what tangled knot of obsession, tightened over the years, had led to this outcome—but I was done. I wasn't there to play some bit part in an asshole's psychodrama.

He looked down at me. "I'll be back soon. We've got a lot to talk about, Jim, unfinished business and opportunity. Remember what we talked about though. Think about *Average Dads.*" He started to make his way to the door, before turning back.

"And maybe reflect a bit on how your writing's going while you're doing it."

He paused, looming over me, fixing me with an expression I'd been seeing my whole life. It was a look, a kind of up-turned sneering hauteur that was near theatrical in its disdain. It had been my father's default expression.

It was one I saw whenever I saw my reflection, the source of my ever-deepening scowl-lines. It was the same expression.

It was like looking into a mirror.

Awareness hit me hard, with a rush of vertigo and clammy hands. His face, it was my fucking face. My mother's chin, my father's eyes. My face. Skinnier, a richer tan, wry instead of bitter but unmistakable. My face.

JD's eyes widened and he started to smile, taking in my stunned expression. "Took you long enough," he said, with a chuckle. He gave me a wink and left.

CHAPTER FIVE

I don't remember leaving the McDonald's, or how I made it to my car. I came to on the highway, driving fast and dodging truckers and RVs, in a fury to get home, back to the Gem-And-I, for answers.

There were no Judsons out front and no one in the lot. Inside my apartment, nothing had changed. My door had been locked and my apartment as disturbed as when I left it. My writing desk was still immaculate: a shoebox, a few pens, a legal pad and an open empty Moleskine. Everything else had the same air of enervated clutter as when I'd left. I went to the box.

Here were "my papers," as I called them—my "material," gathered diligently with the foreknowledge that someday, someone would be archiving and analyzing what I left behind. Here it was, the product of my blackout 20s and my L.A. 30s, my body of work.

It didn't fill the shoebox. It could barely fill a file folder. This handful of pages was all I had to show after all those thousands of hours worth of contemplation and brainstorming, all those daydreams and insights and epiphanies and half-started outlines. There were the short stories I'd started and never finished—just an opening paragraph or a few pages with scrawled notes on the bottom. A half-dozen scraps of doggerel, an attempt at a Phillip Larkin pastiche that seemed closer to plagiarism upon a reread, and a few pages worth of dialogue and scenes from the various novels and screenplays I'd worked over in my mind but had never actually begun. Mostly though, the box was full of index cards, maybe 30 of them. Each had an idea on it, for a short story or a screenplay or a novel or a scene. They were good, full of potential. Any one of them would be an excellent starting point if I wanted to get going on a story.

And there it was, at the very bottom: an index card with time-faded ink.

IDEA: TWO CONTRACTOR PARTNERS DOING WORK AT STARTUP 1990s. CAN BE PAID IN STOCK OR $. ONE GETS RICH OTHER GETS NOTHING. SETS UP YEARS LATER HEIST. MURDER? COEN BROTHERS. "AVERAGE DADS." ETHAN HAWKE/ MARTIN LAWRENCE.

That was all there was to *Average Dads,* just an idea, a few sentences, some fantasy casting, all buried at the bottom of a shoebox. Part of me had expected—maybe even hoped—to have found it missing. That at least would have made some logical sense, given me an explanation for JD's impossible knowledge. Instead, I had nothing but more questions.

I needed to act. I took out the legal pad (pages and pages of doodled squares, not much else) and found a blank page where I could try and make some sense. I started with what I knew.

1: An unknown person has a strong physical resemblance to myself.
2: This person has an interest in me. They showed up at my work and acted coy about our history. They tipped me $250.
3: This person attended Reynolds Academy at some point in the 1990s.
4: They know the plot to a script which I'd always meant to write but never did.

With the facts laid out, I felt a little better about the situation, more in control. There were answers here. Start with the obvious ones:

1: Long-lost sibling?
2: Obsessed psycho from Reynolds (Plastic surgery?!)
3: Weird shit.

I started with "long-lost sibling," running the idea over in my mind. Could Dad have had someone on the side? It's possible, sure it was. My parents were classic alcoholic WASPs, full of repression and swoony on G-and-T's by noon. Dad worked for a publishing company back when that meant something, always flying around the country for junkets and meet-and-greets and book signings. He easily could have met someone while Mom and me were cooling our heels at home.

Was JD my half-brother? It'd explain the physical resemblance, some of the quirks. That expression. But not the Reynolds affectations or the impossible nature of that script.

That's what kept coming back to me: the script. I thought about all those books about the paranormal I'd devoured in my '80s childhood, the *Ripley's: Believe it or Nots!* And *Time-Life's Mysteries of the Unknown*. The books were always full of stories about long-lost twins who were separated at birth, with a section (complete with photos!) featuring twins who reunite and discover that they both worked the morning shifts at their local jack-off factory, had each married blowsy diabetics named Sheena, and had each managed to squirt out two kids named Moppo and Socko. I mean, they weren't peer reviewed, but there were a lot of those stories.

Half-siblings aren't all that uncommon. But a twin, a genetically identical one? That was a real possibility. It could clear up a lot of questions.

Is that what I was dealing with? Some long-lost sibling, ripped from Mom's teat? His genes, our genes, somehow imbued from conception with the plot beats of a screenplay?

It was possible—extraordinarily improbable— but possible. It didn't feel right though. I could believe that Dad had a woman on the side— but Mom? Keeping my absent twin a secret? It didn't make sense.

Dad was an asshole, sure. Truth be told, so was Mom a lot of the time. But she was still my mom. The one who fought back when Dad was drunk and swinging fists; the one who made me special cookies every time there was a class bake sale and Stacy Ketterling's mom made her "famous" macadamia munchers. Back in the '90s severe food allergies, like the one I have to macadamia nuts, were diagnosed, in the playground vernacular, as being "totally gay," with a complicating factor of "wack as shit." Mom always made sure I had some of my own cookies I could eat though, ones that substituted hazelnuts for macadamias. She cared.

I felt a rush of tenderness and warmth for Mom. Even for Dad. It was hard to believe, astonishing really, but I was fast approaching the same age they were when they died, a car crash while Dad was driving them back from some convention. It was late. He was drunk. Then they were dead. I'd soon be older than Mom would ever be.

God, what I wouldn't give to have another one of those cookies. I knew I had the recipe somewhere.

So no, JD couldn't have been a long lost twin. Even if he had been, even if our genes were thrumming in consort like a telegraph wire and exchanging thoughts and script ideas across the country, it still left questions.

Next, I let my paranoia unfurl. I moved on to the next option: obsessed psycho. It wouldn't be the first time I ran into some shithead who'd taken something I said to heart, who'd spent years coming up with the perfect riposte or comeback, only to meet with my blank-faced condescension. It used to happen fairly regularly down at the coffee shop, some asshole frat prick or sorority shrew appearing from my past to settle up. I made a lot of enemies back in my twenties, ones I couldn't even remember today.

But would selling an undergrad a stepped-on eight ball or a stemmy dime bag fifteen years ago result in this kind of obsession? Could even the most devastating putdown or insult at a party cause someone to spend the intervening years plotting revenge? Getting plastic surgery? It didn't pass the smell test. And it didn't explain the Reynolds connection.

I thought back to the life I'd left a year ago, when I was a barista in Los Angeles. After I quit dealing and using most of the hard stuff, I'd found a decent—if blinkered— way of living. I kept people at arm's length, still thinking of them as "material" instead of human beings. I'd begun fertilizing the soil of my misanthropy, secure in the knowledge that whatever literary fruit might grow from that hateful soil would be bright and true, if no less bitter. Most of my "friends" from this period were the day-drunks at my local bars, none of whom I ever spoke with about my writing. The only person who I ever spoke with about writing during this time was Marcia, my one-time co-worker, now-time Bigshot Hollywood Sellout.

Was she involved? I couldn't remember if I'd ever spoken with her about my idea for *Average Dads*.

I went over to the shoebox, found the pages she'd marked with red pen when we did our first (and only) work exchange. Her handwriting was feminine and neat, with wide Lisa Frank loops. I looked at what I'd sent her: the opening pages of a Frederick Forsyth/ Robert Ludlum knockoff about the CIA in Southeast Asia.

I winced a bit while re-reading some of it—some random archaic phrasing and stilted vocab, the occasional overblown prose corralled by the wild commas sprinkled about with no real conception of their purpose. But still, there were some excellent turns of phrase, and the central plot was rock solid. I could recognize that at least: it needed work, but the bones were there. This story had a lot of potential. It really did.

Marcia had thought so too, the pages freckled with hearts and exclamation marks. In my memory, the review hadn't gone well. I recalled her tearing it to shreds with criticism, but, reading it now, I saw nothing but enthusiasm. The sole critique on the bottom was barely a critique, just a question: "But where are *you* in this?"

It was a good question then, and still was now.

CHAPTER SIX

My hand cramped. I'd been scribbling notes in the legal pad while I tried to make sense of everything, trying to bring some order to this chaos. For once, I didn't feel exhausted after a shift. I felt alive and vital.

I needed the sun.

I got up from the desk and threw open the blackout curtains, startling a junior Judson who'd been sweeping out front. I waved to them, then looked back at my room.

In the light of early morning, all the mess I'd been avoiding stood stark and exposed. It's easy to live in filth amidst the darkness, to burrow dopily within crepuscular comfort like a sedated possum. In the appraising light of sober day, the mess was unignorable.

I got to work. I stripped my sheets, folded clothes, did laundry, and cleaned out the car. All the while, my mind kept trying to make connections.

I kept coming back to Reynolds. "JD" had attended the school. There was no doubt, not after the McDPs. I could almost believe that a story idea might be buried in the deep DNA of a lost twin or sibling, but something like "McDouble Penetration" could have only been invented sui generis, springing fully grown from my adolescent head like an Athena made of bad food and pornographic allusion.

It was easy to remember when I coined the phrase, the hysterical laughter all around the table. The admiring adolescent eyes, lidded with envy and awe, staring at me from the shadows

But when I probed closer, deeper, sifting through my memory's bottomless depths, the specifics darted away, those names forever out of reach, vanishing into black and impenetrable fathoms.

I felt a shiver when I considered what else might be lurking down there, in the dark and empty.

I found myself regretting for the first time the fact that I never bought one of those smartphones or even a laptop. Until now, I never had a use for surveillance capitalism or digital Skinner Boxes or any of that other diabolical brain-hijacking nerd shit which had become so ubiquitous. I couldn't imagine Kerouac tapping out *On The Road* on a little glowing screen, or picture Montaigne capturing his irreducible self in status updates. It would have been ludicrous—downright insulting!

But having a smartphone sure would've made this journey easier.

It was noon and I was ravenous as I folded the last of my laundry. The place looked about as good as it had since I'd moved in. I felt a little more in control. The walls felt tight though, like I had doubled in size. I needed to move. I had the sensation there was something inside of me, a massive revelation buried within those abyssal depths of memory and time, a revelation whose shape I was beginning to see. There were answers inside. I just had to unearth them.

I went out to my newly cleaned car and started the engine, letting it idle for a moment while I figured out where to go. The library? Use the computer there to do a little digging? Did Rawpump even have a library? I doubted it. No, I wanted big horizons and the wide blue bowl of the desert sky. I had an unmistakable conviction that I'd find the answers to my questions about JD buried within my memories, not on the internet. There was something I knew. I just couldn't face it yet.

The drive to Nevada's Malpaís National Park is flat and hot under the noonday sun. Before I'd started, I'd stopped off at the nearby Safeway and bought groceries—real groceries, instead of the convenience store crap I usually did. Bread, fresh fruit and vegetables, two rotisserie chickens, and a few other healthy treats. After dropping off the food back at the hotel I headed out, a chicken and a jug of cold brew coffee by my side.

The thermostat read 99° but the AC still worked and I felt fine, real fine. I scanned the radio (a dozen stations of norteño and banda, three right-wing stations preaching gospel and insurrection) before finding Green Day on the oldies station. Why yes, I did have the time to listen to them whine, about nothing and everything all at once.

Green Day faded into Nirvana and the years rolled back, Cobain's plangent desire for his heart-shaped-box freeing synapses that had turned stiff with disuse and despair. Memory sparkled wild on the wide and empty highway as it cut across the wide and empty plain.

Reynolds Academy was (still is, I guess) an all-boys school sited in Dogsboro, the taint of New Hampshire, located between the upthrust of the mountains and the sink of Lake Winnipesaukee. Dogsboro is an ugly pit of ravening townies and racist summer folk, with the rolling greens and nineteenth-century granite bulk of the Academy perched over all.

My father was a Reynolds man. There was never any question I would be too. I hated it at first. I'd had such a sheltered California liberal childhood that I genuinely believed racism and antisemitism were historical relics. Reynolds taught me differently. Here were the old hates, the simple dominance of strong over weak with the ancient prejudices running through.

It coarsened me, it made me mean. But I found strength of my own. I learned that being quick and clever and knowing the weak place to strike had true power. That even the strongest hockey player could be brought low by a well-honed comment implying his dyslexia was caused by chronic masturbation and the absence of a father figure. I dealt with bullies by looking up their parent's names in the school directory and writing long encomiums about their mother's fellatio skills (complete with home phone numbers) on the dorm bathroom walls.

It was cruel, it was base. It was what I had to do. And I thrived. Within six months of matriculation, I went from a cringing little wince of a boy to a Reynolds man through-and-through. Someone full of rough good-humor and assurance, capable of standing up for themselves. I learned the secrets of the suit and tie and the Sperry boat shoe, how to tack and jibe a sail or cradle a lacrosse ball and banter wittily for hours without ever saying a word of substance.

I had Brewster Bradley to thank for all that.

Mr. Bradley had style and savoir faire to spare, a fourth generation Reynolds man whose great-grandfather was among those founding Portsmouth bankers who laundered their slave-trade fortunes into respectability via a grand public school. Despite these stodgy origins, Brewster Bradley was, in the parlance of the time, a "sensitive new-age guy." He was equal parts Boston Brahmin and Phish show bro.

Looking back, he couldn't have been more than a few years out of college. I must be a decade older now than he was then. Funny, that.

Nirvana changed to Smashing Pumpkins, and Billy Corgan's voice reminded me that the year 1979 was closer to "1979" than that song's release was to now. Christ. Those years, all those years. They seemed so ephemeral then, the prelude to great things. Now, listening to alt-rock on the fucking oldies station, I regretted not paying more attention to that "then" if this "now" was my ultimate destination.

Time was a thief, but one that knew how to carry a tune at least. The music was as good as ever.

These siren songs that were the soundtrack to my 90s youth made my memories dance, all the neurons slammed together in a sudden mosh pit of recall. It was like I was still there, and there was a chance that all the intervening years, with all their intervening insults, might simply vanish by the chorus. I blinked away the sudden moisture in my eyes, the road ahead doubling for a liquid second. I was there on the highway and I was there, a freshman once more, in Bradley's classroom.

Bradley, always wearing vintage wool with trim nonchalance, is across from me, leaning on a table. He's asked me to stay late after class. It's freshman year, my first semester, and I still think I can slump and crouch my way into invisibility; cringe and hunch into nothingness, as a way to avoid an errant fist or cutting sneer.

"This was good," he says, holding up our class assignment: 750 words about a childhood memory. "Very good, Mr. Dougherty. This bit here about your parents as, hmm, 'a preening pigeon and a strutting dove.' Nice turn of phrase there."

"Thank you, sir," I mumble, staring at my lap.

"I mean it, Dougherty. Between this and the *Catcher in the Rye* essay, you've shown me real… well, I suppose I can call it a flair for this sort of thing. Some lexical dexterity, as it were." He pauses, looks at me, and then out the window to the New Hampshire autumn. Ancient oaks and ruddy maples blaze crimson and gold, set in a vast crown atop the topaz head of the lake, while high above great clouds are scudding fast across the sky.

"Thank you, sir," I swallow.

"Have you ever heard of a salon, Mr. Dougherty?" Bradley asks.

"Like, for hair and stuff?" I answer.

He smiles, indulgent.

"It's a place to meet for conversation and banter, Mr. Dougherty, just an informal little thing. A chance to develop those intangibilities which cannot be taught. I run one every Friday night, just a few of the boys who appreciate cleverness, mostly from the AP classes. Tomorrow night, 8:00 PM, my house behind Maxwell Hall. You know it, right? Good. You don't have to come, Jim, but I think you should." He squeezes my shoulder and gives me a smile. "Go on then, Jim. You're late for lunch."

That was all I really needed, someone to believe in me. It's amazing what a little external validation can do, what a framework it can provide for self-esteem's striving vine. It helped me grow.

But, over the intervening decades, I'd learned this frame is a brittle one that must be strengthened, lest all the growth collapse. I wondered if that's what was happening to me. Had I stopped writing, stopped hearing I was talented, and then stopped believing it? So that I couldn't write at all? Was I stuck in an ever-tightening feedback loop of curdled ambition and failure?

The sight of a dead coyote on the road, its body smeared by semi wheels, brought me back to the present. The landscape had shifted, away from the yucca and palm of the highway and into the broken black of the malpaís—the Bad Land. The surface of the ground was jagged and mean, the overhangs and spikes of a prehistoric lava flow baked into a pointed cruelty by a thousand years of remorseless sun.

The visitor center was rundown and tired. There were two other vehicles, both RVs, and a small informational display with a sign-in box. A few trails, complete with interpretive signs, snaked into the landscape of the malpaís formation itself. Multiple signs attested to the danger in leaving the path, with grim statistics about those who'd wandered off and been lost forever, ending up as dried-up mummies trapped in forgotten lava holes.

I was where I needed to be.

I threw away the remnants of my chicken and refilled my cold brew jug with icy water from the handpump, then took a moment to position myself. A trail beckoned, one mile to Rabbit Ear Lookout. One mile, an easy walk to a pair of two tall sandstone spires that jutted out from the black sea of lava and danced wavy in the heat. I felt stretched, in two places at once, with part of me a precocious fifteen-year-old at

Reynolds and part of me in the desiccating blaze of my weary middle-thirties.

CHAPTER SEVEN

After five minutes on the trail, that stretched feeling snapped. The wispy Reynolds boy faded away before the actuality of the sun and the bite of the rock. I had no hat, no sunscreen, and old shoes. I was a walking cautionary tale. Despite the discomfort, I didn't turn back. I was no closer to any answers, but I was closer to a destination. That was good enough for now.

I fell into the rhythm of a plodding but determined beat drumming hollow on the boardwalk. Clean sweat poured down my face and my head felt clear. A horned toad watched laconically while a whole wake of turkey vultures wheeled high above me. This was the desert. This is why I came to Rawpump in the first place, to ride the thin line between life and death, the one that's most visible when it stands stark and exposed upon the ancient immensity of the land.

The trail rose slowly, cutting through the frozen rills and spines of the antediluvian lava. Birds whose names I didn't know scattered at my approach as I came to Rabbit Ear Lookout, where a scarred bench and a small sign awaited me. I stood between the two sandstone columns which gave the site its name and looked out over the black petrified ocean of lava baking below the glare of the sun. I imagined a great monolithic rabbit sunk below the lava, its ears breaking the surface and me standing between them. Rather than adrift or unmoored, I felt anchored strong between the stones.

I sat on the bench and looked at the sign. A sliver of information—"habitat to many types of migratory birds and endemic reptiles"—was still legible below the endless scrawl of graffiti. I caught my breath.

My mind returned to Reynolds, again.

It's my sophomore year and there's no sight of that cowering, sniveling self from before. In his place is the new me, swaggering and clever and boisterous. We're in Bradley's house, a faculty cottage, decorated in an explosion of Nepalese souvenirs (Peace Corps vet that he was), tasteful historical artifacts, and just the right amount of bric-a-brac. Bradley's done it up right, like he always does, with a tray of international snack foods, oven-baked cheese bread, and unlimited RC Colas.

The light is low and intimate. The soundtrack is eighties, Billy Idol plaintively echoing the chorus of "Dancing With Myself." Six boys sit in a semicircle of chairs and sofa. Bradley is laid out comfortably, lounging on an Eames. I'm there, all eyes upon me. I'm playing the game.

"Brewster Bradley, a brewer of beers, that old sot, besotted, unclotted….hemophiliac, lilac, violet, purple, Grimace, McDonald's, Shamrock Shake, Mick, Michelob beer, back to Brewing…Brewster Bradley," I finish, to laughter and admiration. It was a simple game we played, a sort of freestyle free-association. The only way to lose was to give in to the filler words (ums, yeahs) or pause. The quality of the free association didn't matter compared to the speed.

"Always with the liquor, Mr. Dougherty," Brewster Bradley says, a half-smile on his face. "You know what they say about liquor, don't you?"

"Not unless you buy her dinner first?" I ask, setting off another round of laughter from the dim and anonymous rest.

"It is a 'great provoker of three things,' isn't it, Jim?" He gives me an unamused look.

"Nose painting, sleep, and urine," I respond, the line from Macbeth coming to me with instant recall. (I was sharp back then, so sharp.)

"Well done Jim! Spot on."

"Out, damned spot?"

"Damned odd, old sport." Bradley laughs, and so do the rest.

These moments, just little ones, stayed with me for so long. Memories like this, from a time when someone could still say "has potential" instead of "had," had the worn familiarity of an old pair of boots molded to the shape of my mind.

With a head shake, I broke my reverie. I wasn't here to reminisce about good times. I was here because I had to be, because someone from those Reynolds days was trying to come back into my life after undertaking a considerable effort to do so. Someone in that dimly remembered audience could have been watching intently, laying down the obsessive grooves which would play out decades later.

The movie-familiar cry of a red-tailed hawk focused my attention on the here and now, and I became dizzily aware that my legs were cramping, that I sat exposed on a sunbaked hilltop. I hadn't done much physical exertion in months, and now here I was, getting heat stroke in the vicious sun. A wave of exhaustion and self-disgust crested. What was I doing? Hell, I could have just stayed at home in the dark and the cool and had another maudlin jerk off to all my "remember whens." The end result would have been the same, and I'd have avoided the sunburn.

I recalled that trapped and restless feeling which had come over me back home, the sense of some great imminent lightning-bolt revelation that had driven me here as if by divine design or subconscious compulsion. And yet, I was still no closer to figuring out any of this essential mystery. Anger replaced the exhaustion, a rich and fruitful rage directed at JD and the way he'd upended my life. What had he told me, before he'd left that McDonald's? "Reflect on your writing?"

My first instinct was a familiar and defensive "fuck that." I hated modern writing, that self-reflective and self-referential self-absorption, those febrile autofictions which read like literary masturbation. I just wanted to tell good stories. And even if my output left something to be desired, I was still here, wasn't I? Working a low-effort job in Rawpump so I could be out here in the desert, living in a damn Cormac McCarthy cover illustration? All so I could write?

I'd been telling myself for so long that it was art, not a nine to five. It couldn't be rushed. I was stoking the engine, paying my dues. The day would come.

Wouldn't it?

CHAPTER EIGHT

I stood, wincing at the cramp. I drank water slowly, pouring some on my head and blinking at the sunburn I'd already developed. I wasn't going to let self-pity and sunstroke take me out. I was doing this asshole's job for him, eating myself up with thought and obsession just because some jerk from my past decided to play a sick prank. I was done.

The trail back went quickly. I didn't dawdle. I was fueled by the frustrated and clawing anger directed at JD and a steadfast certainty that I could end this whole thing on my terms, easily. I just had to stop thinking about this sly prick, stop thinking about all the confusion he had dredged up, with memories of Reynolds and those painfully golden visions of my past, and go back to my life.

I kicked a rock cairn on the trail, trying to hit that horned toad which still stood immobile. Asshole. I wanted this over. I wanted this pissant little mystery finished so I could just forget it.

By the time I made it back to my car my anger had faded, leaving me maudlin and uneasy. I thought of going back to the morning heartburn and the lonely mini-mall nights, the tangled sweaty bedsheets and the thwarted desire of the blank page. I was no closer to an answer than when I'd started, no closer to an explanation for JD's face or his knowledge of my script. I'd marched in the harsh sun and sat beneath its stringent gaze and found no revelation in my memories. I hadn't unlocked the identity of some psycho little snot gushing over my tenth grade charms and embarking on a lifetime of plastic surgery, ideation, and obsession. All I'd seen was myself, again and again. Me at different ages, me at different times, but still.

Me, me, me.

I drove back home as the sun began its fiery fall. Rawpump seemed welcoming for once, the lights of its outskirts a spray of benediction dappled across the hollow darkness of the desert night.

Somewhere on that drive, a new feeling took hold. There was a lightness in my chest, the sense of revelation yet again. What was I doing? For so long I'd been living in the twilight of ambition, that dim space of unrealized potential. "Reflect on my writing"? What was there even to reflect on?

I took the Rawpump exit and saw myself plainly, the unrealized hopes and brittle dreams; the decades standing still in the hopes of an easy way. Determination took hold of me, a certainty. I knew what I wanted to be—what I was always meant to be—and that was a writer. But plenty of people had dreams they never fulfilled, and they lived rich and satisfying lives. Could one of those be me?

One of the LDS churches reared up, a "stake" with a distinctive pillar, which led me to thoughts of the Judsons. They were good people at heart. Believed some stupid shit, sure, but no stupider than any other religion. And at least they seemed happy, the kids always respectful and hardworking and smiling, Ma and Pa the stars of their trite but determined love story. They wanted to save me so badly. Maybe I should let them.

A series of possibilities opened up, the determined feeling in my chest crystalizing into hope. If I could give up JD, could just forget him, what else could I forget? I'd spent my whole life on the dreams of being a writer, the thought that my "someday" would come. But dreams don't mean as much in your late thirties.

Why shouldn't I have a good life? A simple one? I wouldn't have to give up all that much. I could convert easy, get dipped or whatever the Mormons do. And a career, a real one, that I could work towards instead of just pass time at. A real career, a dutiful bosomy wife, a handful of obedient children with ludicrous names. Would it really be so bad?

Once I'd tamed my reflexive scorn, it started to seem downright appealing. I could have a whole lot without giving up very much.

Just my dreams.

By the time I'd pulled up to the Gem-And-I, I was resolved. I'd take the Judsons up on their offer. I'd go for that dinner, meet their friends. Attend their church. I felt a rush of gratitude towards that mysterious asshole JD. He'd done me a favor, really. Forced me to see the things right in front of my face I'd been neglecting.

My eyes and head were painful with sunburn and I was ready for a shower, ready to be washed clean of this strange day and to start anew. It would be a pleasure to forget this whole experience, to chalk up the unexplained elements to time and circumstance and the ineffable oddity that was existence.

I was smiling as I unlocked my door and disturbed an envelope that had been pushed underneath.

I bent down and picked it up. There was no address or postage, just my name, "JAMES DOUGHERTY," written in block capitals. I looked outside at the mostly empty midweek motor court, not seeing anyone I didn't already recognize. Ma and Pa Judson were sitting on a pair of lawn chairs out in front of the manager's office, sharing a pitcher of lemonade while their youngest ones played on the asphalt, spotlit by the big sodium-arc lights. I walked over, envelope in hand.

"Good evening James," Ma Judson said in her understated and sturdy manner when I approached. The Judsons were around my age, both in their mid-thirties, but their children and responsibility aged them up so that I always wanted to give them a formal term of address.

"Good evening to you, ma'am." I held up the envelope. "I saw this under my door and wonder if you can tell me who put it there?"

"Oh sure can, Jim," Pa enthused. "Todderdiah did it, right after school. He was meant to have done it earlier in the morning, before he left, but you know how the little ones are. I hope it wasn't too much of a problem, was it?"

"Wouldn't say 'too much' Mr. Judson. Just about the right size."

"But you never told us you had a brother, James!" Ma Judson exclaimed. "Vackenzie said he looked just like you. She was working the nightdesk when he showed up and she just couldn't believe it! Said she darn near had kittens! Was the note too late?" Ma looked worried. "I told Vackenzie to drop it off herself! But she was running late to morning practice—varsity this year, y'know—and well, I guess she gave it to Todderdiah and he just plum forget. I'm so sorry. I should have checked."

My throat dried up. All the thoughts I'd been having earlier, the ones about taking the Judsons up on their offer, scattered off to join the bats dipping and weaving between the parking lot lights.

"Thank you, and thank the young'uns. It's fine. My brother and me, uh, we've been out of touch for a while." I had to master the urge to walk away from them immediately, to tear the envelope open and see what it contained.

Ma Judson's face screwed up in sympathy. "Families are forever, James. It's true. Did Pa tell you about Beverly Anderson? She's such a sweet girl. It's so hard to be alone. Do you ever find that to be so, James?"

I made a non-committal murmur, eager to leave but trying not to be rude. A wave of disgust came over me, disgust at the cornfed sincerity of these deeply blinkered people with their provincial satisfaction at their narrow little lives. Give up my dreams, my destiny, for what? For the joys of sitting hand-in-hand in a motor court, watching a flock of brats play earnest games in the harsh fluorescent glare?

I thanked them, made my excuses, and left.

I came back to my apartment and marveled a bit at the cleanliness, grateful to my earlier self for putting in the work. After a few deep breaths, I opened the envelope. Inside were two paperback pages, each ripped out of a different mass market edition. On top was a Post-It note.

"Figured you'd still have questions. Maybe these can help. You can do this."

I waited another moment before looking at the paperback pages, aware I was mentally poised above a deep abyss and that I could fall so easily—fall forever—into the dull disorienting plunge of madness or despair. It wasn't the first time. I'd had moments like this before, the axial ones where it seemed like my whole life might hinge on the outcome. I'd always lingered in those last seconds of flux, preferring that potential to the harsh surety of truth. None of those moments were pleasant, but there was a lot more comfort in the potential than in the certainty. There was the pause after the policeman had asked if I was the son of Tom and Dorothy Dougherty and whether or not they drove a Volvo; that long afternoon holding the thick final letter of expulsion from Reynolds, unsure whether or not to open it at all; unfolding the note Marcia had left for everyone in the coffee shop, paralyzed by the possibility that there might be something more in it for me besides "goodbye and good luck."

I shook off the mental cobwebs and took a few deep breaths. I was tired of waiting. I needed to know. I started to read.

The first page was yellowed, from a book that felt at least a decade old. I scanned it quickly, then slowly, and again. Denial and disbelief clashed with outrage as the words sunk in. The page (front and back) was an excerpt of a scene set in a bar in Northern Thailand. The bar was owned by a retired American pilot who'd fought in the Laotian secret wars, smuggling opium and weapons to the hill tribes. The man was maudlin and drunk—consumed by regrets and the blood on his hands—when he was approached by a junior CIA agent. The junior agent had a proposition for him concerning the whereabouts of 50 kilos of Royal Lao gold that had been hidden in the jungle for sixty years.

The writing was terse and noir, the second page ending with, "'There are no kings and queens left in Laos, Frank, they shot them in a cave. Here there's only men. And men have needs. Expensive ones.'" At the top of the page was "*Quoth the Raven*... Page 65" and on the back it said "James Dougherty... Page 66."

I put the page down and tested myself. That looming revelation which had pursued me into the desert, that had chased me into the badlands, was here. I looked upon it. This was my novel, sure as hell was. It was a novel I'd been writing in my head since I was a teenager and read my first Frederick Forsyth. This was no fake. Even if I dismissed JD's knowledge of my script as a remarkable piece of cold-reading expanding on a stolen index card, I couldn't dismiss this. The papers were as real as could be, the cheap paper worn thin, with the light sheen of finger oils that spoke of constant handling. Every sentence felt both novel and familiar, like when you reread something you'd written while drunk.

This was real. It wasn't an expert forgery commissioned by a bedeviled sophomore who had spent twenty years trying to become me, nor was it the product of a lost sibling with the same name. It was real. It was mine.

But I had never written it.

The second page was different. I could see hints of my bitter voice but it'd been softened into wry irony. Every word of *Quoth The Raven* had echoed for me, a familiarity born of a hundred daydreams. But this was new.

It was mostly a dialogue between a man and a woman in their sixties, a pair of English professors somewhere small but prestigious. The two had been having an affair since Reagan, a quiet but passionate love kept on the margins of their real lives, in faculty retreats and holiday getaways. Now the woman's husband had died while the man's wife was starting to show signs of dementia, and the two must decide what comes next. The dialogue sparkled, both light and funny and heartbreakingly elegiac. The top of the page read *"Auld Acquaintances…. Page 12"* and the back said "Ibanez/ Dougherty…. Page 13."

The revelation stood exposed, adamant in its certainty. JD wasn't some obsessive from my past, nor was he a genetic fluke. He was me and I was him. JD was James Dougherty.

The force of the revelation staggered me, left me feeling dissociated and rueful, aware of the denial which had kept me from seeing the truth. The room spun all around me and I had to sit down.

But after the initial shock, I discovered a deeper strata of certainty. I had already known, hadn't I? Part of me must have known, right from that first glimpse. I didn't want to see it, I couldn't see it. I wasn't able.

I had work in a few hours, but the thought of going seemed impossible. Tiredness from the hike, the long lingering aftereffects of sunbaked exertion, and the aftershocks of my new awareness left me dazed.

I picked up the phone and called in to the Deuces, telling them I was sick and would miss my shift. Eduardo was pissed, but Eduardo was always pissed. Afterwards, I felt calm and I felt certain. I took the legal pad off my desk. I crossed out the first two entries and looked at the third.

1: ~~Long lost sibling~~
2: ~~Obsessed psycho from Reynolds (plastic surgery?!)~~
3: Weird shit

Despite the dissonance, I started to smile. Weird shit? I could work with that.

That night I dreamt of boats again, of lonely frightened ships. Two vessels tugged across an ashy sea that roiled below a wine-red sky. They weren't lost anymore, though. They knew where they were going.

CHAPTER NINE

The next few weeks were a blur. I spent my days in preparation and every shift in anticipation. I made it out to Vegas on the weekends to visit the public library, spending entire days reading and copying everything I could find on the ethnographic folklore of the mysterious double.

There were two primary mythological depictions of the "double" in my research that I summarized roughly as '"the good" and "the bad." The phenomenon was an ancient one, with examples from the folklore of many diverse cultures. Literature abounded on the topic, touching on everything from the atavistic and chthonic depictions of myth, where the figure is a frightening and enigmatic portent, to the 19th-century tropes of romantic literature, where the double can represent the repressed self or the wistful longing for a life that had never been lived. In other cultures, the double was the guiding figure of the afterlife, the divine heavenly apparition who appears to aid the transition to death and the underworld.

In most of the Western canon, the double was a doleful figure associated with tragedy, firmly linked to "the bad." The double is usually met only briefly, with their appearance foretelling some personal disaster or impending death. In Germany, this forbidding apparition was called the "doppelgänger," while in the Irish and Anglo traditions, the unlucky figure was known as the "fetch," a supernatural harbinger of doom that dated back to pre-modern folklore. It was a sinister piece of myth.

On the other end of the scale was "The Ka." In ancient Egypt, this represented the individual's vital essence, the pure soul-self, which could sometimes walk on the earthly plane alongside the physical body, offering a glimpse of the divine-essence in the drab mundane. This was the "good" option.

My research didn't give me any definitive answers. There simply weren't any to find. But one of the few threads that seemed to bind all these different myths, cultural expressions, and archetypes was this: seeing your double never ended well. In almost every case, it ended in death.

JD's appearance in my life hadn't seemed to coincide with any particular misfortune. Nor did he seem liminal, a psychopomp sent to shepherd my soul onward.

Still, it didn't hurt to prepare for that possibility.

While tapping out my queries on the Vegas library research computer—in between a sour-smelling bum and the dazed asshole wearing slept-in Brooks Brothers who was frantically googling variations of "how to count cards"—I had a revelation. Seeing JD for what he was hadn't made me want to submit meekly to death, to await his ushering touch so that I might pass on in a blaze of symbolism in accordance with some ancient mythos. It made me want to kick his ass.

I wasn't ready to be some placeholder patsy, some abject lesson in unfulfilled potential. JD was a challenge, one that I would have to deal with in order to keep my place in the world.

The knowledge that there was only room for one of us on life's big wide stage fuelled me up, kept my focus. I wasn't the understudy, the shadow-self or the fetch. I was me, not him. My life wasn't perfect but it was mine, every fucking second and every goddamn breath.

And I wanted to keep it that way.

Armed with the fruits of my research, I started to prepare for our next meeting. I made purchases all across Nevada in the process of securing some mystical protections mentioned in the primary sources, trying my damnedest not to scoff at the checkout. I'd reached a state of equilibrium within, holding space for two possibilities that felt equally real: I was either showing signs of incipient paranoid schizophrenia or I might have to destroy, exorcise, or bind some type of supernatural entity.

By the end of that month, I was as ready as I could get. I kept the trunk of my car full of a wide array of specially prepared or recently purchased items and just kept marking time.

Finally, after two more weeks, I stopped expecting him. I began to settle into my rut again. My eyes began to dim. I considered how to get myself diagnosed and treated for delusional mental illness while still keeping my casino license.

And then, on a Thursday just after midnight, he was there.

I had been sitting alone at a dead blackjack table—empty—before he showed up, walking casual. He was wearing green now, a rich forest blazer worn over another tight black shirt and jeans.

Now that I knew what to expect, what to look for, the identification seemed obvious. He was me. But different. The face had an openness which I had never cultivated, a relaxed cast to his features where my default was a scowl. He had the look of a winner, an effortless ease that showed in smile lines instead of crow's feet. He was thinner but his hair was thicker and had the bottle-dark of "Just for Men."

It became clearer to me why I hadn't recognized JD at first, why it had taken me so long. In my mind's eye, I was still that Reynolds kid: the fast, young, un-coarsened by time 16-year-old. And I have never taken a "selfie" in my life. I keep my mirror sessions professional, sticking to the stains and slop.

I understood why it had taken me so long to recognize the obvious: I'd spent years avoiding my own gaze.

Now that gaze was unavoidable as I stared into my own eyes, sitting across from me at the table.

"Hello," he said.

"Hello yourself," I replied,

"Hmmm… something like that." He gave me a teasing smile. "Hello ourself."

"Something like that," I answered, not giving an inch. "So what's the play?"

"Blackjack, isn't it?" He put down a fifty dollar chip. "I'm in."

I gave him a long stare, then pushed the chip back to him and off the table. I shuffled the cards slow, by hand, and picked up the cards I wanted after a long lazy fan. With casual ease I dealt us both dirty, the cards face-up.

I gave us each a pair of aces, the best deal you can get in blackjack. JD gave me a frank and admiring look; I could tell he liked my style.

I knew what I was doing would mean the end of my job at the Deuces. It could mean the end of my gaming license. You don't fuck with the deal, you don't fuck with the bet. That's unforgivable.

I didn't care. I'd been planning this moment too long. I wanted flair, I wanted savoir faire. I wanted… *symbolism*. "Your move," I told him.

He looked at the cards, looked at me and gave a real smile, an understanding one. "You always split aces? They can go two ways, right?"

"They're worth either a one or an eleven," I answered. "The value is up to the player—and the play. When you're dealt a pair, you have the option to split them into two hands and then get dealt two new cards. That's your best bet for a 21."

"So the cards have the potential for both values." JD gave his little chuckle. "All that changes is circumstance and play."

"A lot can depend on circumstance."

"Even more depends on the player."

"Maybe, when you've been dealt a good hand."

"Plenty of people with bad hands win big."

We paused for a moment. I was smiling, braced. I couldn't help enjoying myself—both of them.

Eduardo came up, flanked by a security guard. He wasn't smiling. "You're done," he said.

"Why's that, Eduardo?" JD asked, squinting at the nametag.

"I don't know what the fuck kind of scam the two of you are running, but you're done. Jim, you're fired. Look at the table, look at your goddamn hand. We're going to be reviewing tapes and checking totals. We will prosecute your ass if the count is off by a dime," Eduardo fumed.

"No you won't," I answered. "I'm done here." I stood up. "I'm done with this bullshit job and this bullshit life. Check the fucking tapes, check the fucking chips. I'm pristine." I pushed my way past Eduardo and the security guard, a cirrhotic retired cop who made a half-hearted tug at my jacket. I kept going, JD a few paces behind.

All around the casino, DOGs bobbed their heads and whispered, growling at my disgrace. Eduardo was in a tense conversation over the walkie-talkie with the manager on duty. I didn't care. I was clean but I was done. "Wait here," I said to JD before going into the employee lounge. He just shrugged. I grabbed my bag from my locker and left.

Eduardo and the cop tailed the two of us out into the parking lot. I ignored them. They couldn't detain me and they had nothing on the tapes that could get me in trouble. I hadn't taken JD's bet when I dealt us both pairs of aces. The round hadn't started so there was no fraud. No harm, no foul.

It was still dark in the parking lot, no hint of an easterling glow. The sodium-arc lights—haloed by fuzzy manes of moths and hungry bats—gave JD a washed-out, corpselike pallor. The adrenaline of the last twenty minutes faded, leaving me shaky and anxious. I unlocked my car and we both got in.

"Where we headed?" JD asked.

"Headed out," I answered, turning on the car.

He gestured to the desert night. "Your move."

I shifted into drive. "Your play."

CHAPTER TEN

We drove out into the dark. It was just the two of us. The highway was wide and empty, the night broken only by the sporadic twin-deaths of headlights blurring past.

"Ka? Clone? Or fetch?" I finally asked.

JD laughed, a long and honest one. "Ka? Fetch? I genuinely have no idea what you mean."

"A Ka. The Egyptian second self," I said, a little sheepishly. "The soul that walks."

"Well, someone has been at the library!" JD said, still chuckling. "The only Ka I know comes from crows."

"Clone?"

"Who on earth would want to clone you? And why?"

"Fetch," I muttered.

"You tossing?"

"No, a fetch. A supernatural double. Seeing one is an omen of impending death or disaster."

"Well, you saw me, what, a month ago? Any impending deaths or disasters?" JD said, more seriously.

"The night is still young," I spat.

"I owe you an apology," he answered after a moment. "This has been a very strange experience for me—I'm sure you can relate. But I shouldn't have come at you the way I did. There were better ways. I guess I just got caught up in the novelty. You know how we are, always looking for the clever banter and the joke, the big *beau geste*. It gets in the way, you know, us never coming to the point. But that was wrong. I shouldn't have played you the way I did. I owe you more than that."

"I appreciate that," I said, and meant it. "There's not really a good etiquette guide for when you meet your fetch."

"Stop trying to make 'fetch' happen," JD laughed. "It's not going to happen."

I gave the reference the smile it deserved and kept on driving.

The truth was between us, plain as the noses on my faces. But I wouldn't be the one to broach it. The only piece of good advice my father ever gave me was "act like you've been there before." Sure, I was newly unemployed and barreling down a pre-dawn desert highway with my doppelgänger riding shotgun, but there was no reason not to be cool about it. I let the silence hold.

We pulled into the all-night trucker diner on the outskirts. The "Snake Eyes Diner" is a clean, well-lighted place and doesn't skimp on the portions, making up with quantity what they lack in quality. And after all, a trucker coming off a 15 hour run, powered by Adderall and chewing tobacco, doesn't tend to be picky.

I chose it because I knew it would be full of people, even at this hour. Despite the ease of our banter, I wasn't ready to be alone together. Not yet. We sat across from one another at a booth and waited in silence for the waitress to arrive.

I stared at JD while JD stared right back at me. I felt a reflexive urge to look away but instead I held the reflection of my other self.

"Weird as hell, isn't it?" JD said at last. "Absolutely weird."

"Weird shit," I confirmed. "Very weird."

The waitress arrived with bags under her eyes and a pot of lukewarm coffee. "What'll it be, fellas?"

JD and I looked at one another. I wasn't in the mood for the playful banter, the elaborate routine we'd done in McDonalds. The preamble was over. It was time to get to business.

"Pancakes, double-sta—" JD and I both said at once, in unison. We stopped, gave one another a look.

The waitress smiled. "Ain't that funny? My sister and I are the same way, always getting in one another's path. Which of you is visiting and which one lives here?"

I motioned for JD to go ahead. "I'm visiting," he said. "Been awhile."

"Too long," I agreed.

"Double-stack pancakes come with two eggs, any style, and bacon or sausage. What'll be?" she asked.

"Scrambled and bacon," we said in unison again. The waitress left, chuckling.

"Just to get this out of the way," I started when she was out of earshot. "You're not my long-lost identical twin, are you?"

"Well, let's see," JD began, rolling up a jacket arm and sleeve to reveal a jagged scar across the back of his left arm. I rolled up my own sleeve and put it down on the table to compare. They were the same, the result of falling off a tree and onto a rake when I was nine years old.

"Christ," I said. "Remember Stacy Ketterling?"

"Uggh," JD groaned, "with her mom's poisonous cookies and that goddamn rumor she spread about the scar."

"Spoiled little bitch," I concurred. Stacy had gotten it into her mind that I was faking it about the bake sale, pretending an allergy to her mom's macadamia munchers for the attention. She'd then decided to tell everyone that the scar on my arm was the result of some kind of masturbation incident. The last few months of eighth grade everyone called me "Wanken-stein."

"God, felt great to get back at her though, didn't it?" JD asked me.

That first break back from Reynolds, I'd seen a few of my middle-school friends hanging out in one of their basements. Stacy was there. I told everyone that I knew "a joke so funny, it'll knock your tits off," then paused a moment before continuing with, "but it looks like Stacy's already heard it." There was a moment of stunned silence before the room erupted in cruel whoops. I beamed as she stormed out, crying, and I had my revenge.

Never saw any of that crowd again, though.

"It did feel good," I agreed.

I took a beat and thought about the further implications, the fact that we shared an identical past but had clearly diverged at some point after Reynolds Academy. There was a reason for the confidence, the assurance, the changes in our physical appearance. I wanted to know.

"You ready to cut the shit?" I asked.

"Born ready," JD replied. "We've got a lot to talk about."

"You got the time?" I asked him.

"I've got plenty. A full twelve hours and—" He pulled out his smartphone and looked at the time. "We've only spent a couple of them."

"Why do you use that thing?" I pointed at the smartphone. I hated the fucking devices, those addictive-surveillance boxes.

"It's handy," he shrugged. "Has a full library on it, all my books. All my photos. My whole life."

"Let's talk about those books, shall we?" We were finally getting to the meat of it, those mystery paperback pages and that impossible script.

"Oh, I'm sure we'll get around to it." JD was evasive. "Do you write?" he said, changing the subject.

I paused before answering. "I'm a writer."

"But do you write?" he pressed.

"Now and again." I took a moment. "Nothing published though, not for a long time."

"Since Reynolds?"

"Since Reynolds."

"What happened at Reynolds?" JD asked me.

"What do you mean?"

"Did you graduate?"

"Not from Reynolds," I answered. "Did you?"

"No." He shook his head. "Expelled junior year."

"Plagiarism?"

"Plagiarism."

It comes back quickly, that queasy feeling in my gut at the word "plagiarism."

I'm back in Brewster Bradley's faculty cottage, two years older and now a junior. I've filled out, no longer just a shadow of a thing. Raw stubble itches on my chin. I hate shaving.

I'm fighting back tears, fighting back against the drop in my stomach, the disappointment in Brewster's eyes. He's holding one of my essays. On the table in front of him is the senior thesis I stole it from.

"Don't you have anything to say about it, Jim? Anything at all?"

I had a million things to say. It was just a stupid assignment: "2000 words on the theme of duality in Shakespeare's *Sonnets*." It wasn't that it was hard, not really, not with two weeks to do it. I'd procrastinated too long, but I figured I could just put something quick and dirty down about fair youths and dark ladies and all the other things about Shakespeare I already knew. It could've been done, would've been easy. Would've been a solid C. Would've changed everything.

But then Friday afternoon beckoned from the window of my dorm room, with a view of the thawing pools atop the hard ice of Lake Winnipesaukee. They were beautiful, those pools, reflecting the lambent light of the dipping sun in a slow and rippling aurora. I'd sat at my table and watched until the darkness swallowed all and the stars began to wheel.

Next it was Saturday, and wouldn't you know it? One of the kids in the dorm got a big package of VHS tapes his brother had made for him, most of a *X-Files* season and a whole grip of *Seinfeld* and a few other things. He put them on in the television room and that took us until Sunday afternoon before we reached the nadir of Jerry Springer reruns and I broke free.

The assignment was due on Wednesday. I still had two days to get something written. But Monday flew by in a blur, and then it was Tuesday and I hadn't started. And there was a new episode of *Frasier* on Tuesday night. I had a deadline.

So, I only had a few hours to get it all finished. I still could have just sat down and done it and still could have gotten that C. But the truth of it was that I didn't just want a passing grade. I wanted to *shine.*

I was on the top floor of the library. The walls of cold granite, quarried under Rutherford B. Hayes, leeched the energy and warmth right out from me. And the thought of sitting there for two more hours, my breath visible in the air, left me weak. Left me looking at the surrounding shelves.

Reynolds seniors spend their year writing a capstone, a kind of thesis. And Reynolds was proud of its capstones. The library held thousands of them, printed and bound and collated on index cards. No one ever went into them, because who really cared what some squinty asshole from the 1930s had to say about Flaubert or fractions or French? I was just procrastinating when I got up from the desk and walked over to the card catalog, still procrastinating as I started flipping through them—Scholasticism (Medieval), Shaka Zulu (Anglo-Zulu War), Shakers (19th century→ Era of Manifestations)—and then it was Shakespeare. Card after card for Shakespeare. Another minute flipping and then, right after Shakespeare (sonnets→ Didactic) was Shakespeare (sonnets → Duality).

Then I was in the shelves and then I was at the capstone and then it was at my desk and the new episode of *Frasier* was a few hours away. It all felt so pointless, a lark. I knew I had talent and knew I was smart and so did Brewster Bradley... we were friends. What did it matter if I copied out a few paragraphs and examples from some dumb thirty-year-old essay? I'd had a short story published only last month after Bradley encouraged me to submit to his old college lit journal. I was now a legitimate published author. So why not? Honestly, it felt like a joke, but one played on the slower students. Not the ones like me.

So, before too long, the essay was done and my evening was mine once more. I handed it in the next morning and by Friday I was in Bradley's cottage.

I was already on thin ice at Reynolds. My math grades stunk and the snark I'd developed pissed a lot of people off. I'd been on academic probation since the new term. But that's the thing about thin ice: you never know how thin it is until it breaks. You can skate as fast as ever and not know until it's too late.

I was never really worried. I was the star of Bradley's salons, my story had been published in a real literary journal, and I'd done exceptionally well on my verbal PSATs. You can get a lot of leeway as long as you're exceptional. Who cared about my math grades? Or chemistry? Or Spanish? Who cared if I got write-ups for back talk? I was going to be a writer, and none of that mattered.

But now the ice is breaking all around, and what I feel is that sudden frozen plunge.

"Well Jim, what do you have to say?" Bradley isn't going to let me slouch into my seat, to mutter my way through this.

"It was just a stupid essay!" I explode. "About Shakespeare. Another dead white guy. Who cares what I have to say about him?"

"It's not about the essay, Jim, it's about the plagiarism. Reynolds has an honor code." Bradley is so disappointed in me, his heart is breaking and so is mine. Hot tears roll down my cheek. I push them away angrily.

"So fucking what are you going to do? Get me expelled? You're going to do this to me?" I'm hyperventilating.

"I don't have a choice." He pauses for a moment. "Maybe this is what you need Jim, a wake-up call. Cleverness and surface charm will only get you so far in life. You need to work, to really work. You can't cut corners with slapdash efforts, can't expect to skate by on the bare minimums or the easy way. You need to persevere. Otherwise you'll do this again and again, take the easy way. You did this to yourself, Jim," Bradley sighs. He rubs a spot between his eyes. "You're your own worst enemy."

CHAPTER ELEVEN

Facing myself in the diner, 20 years later, the moment stretched between the decades and the two of us, a warp of memory and shame and guilt woven across the dusty weft of age. We each gave our other self a long and penetrating stare. No one ever really knows what another person has experienced. No man can carry another's burden. No one knows what it's truly like to be someone else. Except, in this case, we did and we could. The thought seemed to come to both of us at the same time, a connection and an intimacy so real and so intense it left me slightly dizzy and choked with emotion. Here was someone who'd felt exactly what I'd felt, who'd known exactly what I'd done. Who had lived what I lived. Here was someone who knew, who finally truly *understood*.

I think if we'd sat there for another minute, we both might have started crying.

Our food arrived in a rush of charm and commotion, and the moment passed. We wiped our eyes surreptitiously (checking to see if the other had noticed and was doing the same), and JD thanked the waitress. She filled our cups with coffee, leaving the two of us with our breakfasts.

"Do you ever think of Brewster Bradley?" I inquired. "Because I have. Lately I've been thinking of him quite a bit."

JD paused, the fork of eggs halfway to his mouth, and waited a moment before continuing. "Brew? Yeah, I think of him. Saw him just last month in Burlington." He said it casually but with an affect I recognized. He was keeping something from me, trying to be nonchalant. Sneaky. But I knew him all too well. In an instant that warm feeling of intimate connection severed, and I felt overwhelmed by anger.

"Brew, huh? Sounds like you two have gotten close." My voice was a little too wild, a little too loud. I reeled it in, tried for that same casual indifference as JD. "But maybe you can help me answer this question: how have you guys gotten so close when I haven't spoken with him in 20 years?"

He took another moment, taking a long sip of his coffee. "Enough foreplay, huh?" he asked, after a break. I didn't answer. "Well, alright. But here's how this is going to go, Jim. We can get it on, but it takes two to fuck. Otherwise it's just masturbation."

"Yet here we are." I waited a beat. "Playing with ourselves in public."

"A truly bad habit—we'll end up with hairy knuckles and squinty eyes." JD laughed, playfully. "Alright, let's do this quid pro quo. I'll answer some questions, then you answer mine. I'll start with the answers. How familiar are you with DARPA?"

"Familiar enough," I responded, after thinking about it for a minute. "That weird sci-fi Department of Defense shit, right? Killer robots and amoral AI and drones that can safely blow up a wedding from 50,000 feet?"

"There's that, yes. But they work quite a bit with fiction writers. Did you know that? They've done it since Asimov in the 1950s. DARPA is a program where the people who imagine the future collaborate with the people who make it real. They've built the world we live in."

"And a great fucking job they've done," I replied. "Clearly they've made the world a better place. No problems with unchecked social media, with algorithmic brainwashing, climate change, and all the—"

"Hey, I get it man," he interrupted, holding up a finger. "You're preaching to the choir here. No one is ever going to agree with you more. They are the vanguard of the 21st century's diseased neoliberal techno-dystopia, right? Is that what you expect me to say? Because I can, easy."

"So, you're what? Some Department of Defense clone?" I'd read a bit about DARPA, knew it was a place of black budgets and unspeakable experimental skunkworks. They could clone someone easily enough, but sending that clone out rattling through the desert with a pocket full of cash and a series of garishly colored blazers in order to harass the original seemed like a stretch.

"I told you before, Jim, no one wants to clone you. No one really cares." JD pushed the plate back. He'd only taken a few bites. His plate was mostly full. Mine was mostly empty. The pancakes were good.

JD stared off and thought for a minute before continuing. "The Department of Defense is an immoral institution. But like any institution, it's made up of people. After *Fermi's Echo*—"

"*Fermi's Echo?*" I interrupted. "My book about the aliens?"

"Our book."

"But I've never written a goddamn word of it!"

"Jimmy, Jimmy, Jim. I'm trying to do this right and you're all over the place. How did I get here? Via DARPA. You want more details? Wait your fucking turn." There was real anger on JD's face. "Now it's mine. When was the last time you wrote something and actually finished it?"

I opened my mouth then closed it. It was a good question. I could barely remember the last time I actually finished something. "It's been a while," I admitted.

"Do you still have those index cards? Those ideas?"

"A whole stack of them."

"Tell me the last one you wrote."

I had to close my eyes and think about it. I'd jotted something down just last week after one of the library trips—an idea about those two ships I'd been dreaming of, the lost ones adrift on the evil-looking swells. "There're two men trapped on a lifeboat with sharks all around them," I started. "One of them is a rich sociopathic passenger from the first class cabins, the other is a deckhand. It's a slow-motion cat-and-mouse game between the two of them, a subtle battle of poisons and wits and eventual cannibalism. I'd call it *Time and Tide.*"

JD was nodding. "I like it, maybe kind of a close-third from the perspective of the deckhand? Hmm…maybe a real slow-moving but suspenseful narrative with a lot of internal digressions? Man versus man and man versus nature?" He was smiling. "I can see it now. A nasty little book, with a nasty little twist at the end."

"Can't forget about the twist." I smiled back, but then it faded. "It'd be hard to write, though. I'd need to find the time, really need to let the story idea ferment for a bit before I can bottle it."

The waitress came and took our plates, squinting at JD's. "Something wrong with your breakfast, hon?"

"It was genuinely superlative. I'm afraid I don't have too much of an appetite." JD gave a winning smile, one I remembered from long ago. That smile died as the waitress left, and he turned his attention back to me. "How much time would you need to write the story, Jim?"

I felt the procrastinator's panic set in. "Hard to say, really. Could do it with, oh, a few months, maybe? If I were on some kind of writer's retreat, somewhere I wouldn't have many obligations."

"Do you have all that many obligations now? Are you broke?"

"Well, I'm out of a job. I'm not going back to the Deuces, that's for sure. Odds are that I cost myself my casino license tonight. But yeah, I do have something squirreled away." I thought of my bank account, the expenses hitherto limited to the cheap extended stay rent and convenience store forays. I surprised myself by realizing that I'd put away quite a nice little nest egg over the past year. I actually could take a few months off and be fine. I could make things happen.

"So what's holding you back from writing that story?"

There it was, the question which had dogged me over the last two decades. Why the hell hadn't I finished something? Anything at all? Why was it all just false-starts and jotted down ideas and a heap of potential that was starting to fester? The voice in my head—that old procrastinating beguiler—spoke up in its lugubrious tone: "you can't rush art," it whispered. "You know how good you are, why do you need anyone else's approval? And the publishing market these days... It's so bad. The kids don't read. No one does. And good luck getting an agent with a first draft. You need something perfect, something fully formed and perfect. Just relax and let it happen. It will. Someday..."

That voice, as familiar to me as my own, now grated. I didn't want to listen to its whine. I didn't want to hear it at all.

"My turn," I answered, after a brief and bitter reflection. "What the hell does DARPA have to do with you being here? And how does it all actually work?"

There was that beat, then the wry chuckle of JD's I was starting to resent. "Alright, I get it. You want to know the rules, right? Can't enjoy a story without knowing all the rules. Is there anything worse than that magical realism shit where things just happen?" He collected his thoughts before continuing. "Well, here we go."

CHAPTER TWELVE

"Like I was saying," JD continued, "DARPA is an immoral institution, but the people who work there are like anyone else, a complicated mixture. I ended up with some fans there, after uh…some projects of mine turned out well."

"You're talking about *Silicon Daddy?*" I asked, starting to feel the pieces slot into place.

JD laughed. "No, that was just some hack shit. They neutered the hell out of it. But *Quoth The Raven* had some big fans in the black-bag brigade, a few old spooks who'd appreciated the sympathy of my portrayal. That got me on their radar. And then *Fermi's Echo* was such a hit that I ended up taking a pass on the new *Star Wars* script."

"*Star Wars?*" I interrupted.

"*Star Wars,*" JD confirmed. "And everybody loved those movies. Nerds are easy to please, y'know? Well, after that things really started cooking for me. I got invited to do some classified TED Talk type bullshit to the geeks in the basements. Some army conferences. I made a few friends, a good first impression. And, well, DARPA is just a bunch of the biggest geeks in the world—with access to untraceable billions and no real oversight."

"Sounds just great," I replied. "The future in the hands of maladjusted sociopaths."

"Same as it always was, Jimmy. Same as it always was." He stopped for a minute, started to take another sip of water before checking himself and putting down the glass. We made eye contact and I felt that eerie unmooring yet again. "You ready?" he asked. I nodded.

"The official name is the Schrödinger Entanglement Experiential Device—SEED for short— but everyone just calls it the 'Might've Box.'"

"Schrödinger? Like that zombie cat in the box?" I asked. I had a vague recollection of a thought experiment, something about a living animal sealed away from sight in a dark box—existing in an undefined state of both alive and dead, just passing time.

JD nodded. "Yup, the same guy. The one behind that dead-cat thought experiment. I am not going to bog us down with a bunch of half-remembered jargon, but the gist of it is that he and his physicist buddies had a real revelation back in the 1910s about the nature of conscious observation. It's real spooky shit, you know? Turns out, the act of looking at a subatomic particle changes that particle. Simply seeing something changes it. In that cat scenario, the box also has a Geiger counter which will release poison if it detects radioactivity—the twist is, until someone opens the dark box and looks for themselves, the Geiger counter can't detect a thing. So the cat is nothing but potential, frozen in a state of living death."

"How?" I answered, thinking about that paralyzed half-existence of permanent waiting with a shudder.

"No one knows how—but it's true. The best they've figured out is that somehow these particles—the things that make up everything— can theoretically exist in multiple states at once—as both the 'either' and the 'or'—in what they call a superposition, until such time as someone observes them. Then the state becomes fixed."

"Yeah, I get you. The fix is in, right?" I replied.

JD rolled his eyes, made a rueful little noise that might have been a laugh or a sigh. "Didn't anyone ever tell you being a cynic is overrated?"

"I'd tell you that it takes one to know one, but then we'd really just be going in circles."

"You done?"

I nodded, abashed, and JD proceeded.

"Okay, so what all this tells us is that the subatomic particles, the very building blocks of existence, are somehow shaped by perception. How you see the world changes it—it's a new world every time you open your eyes."

"Oh bullshit. That's just quantum solipsism," I said, wearily. "Enough with the metaphors." I gave him back the same rueful laugh, knowing he'd be sure to find it as annoying as I had. "Why not move on to the practicalities, huh?"

JD nodded. "That's fair. So one day in the late 1990s, this thing just appeared in one of the Pentagon basements. Poof. A big-ass doorframe wired up to some huge humming particle-accelerator-looking-motherfucker, complete with an instruction manual."

"Alright, I get it," I answered. "Magic door. Different worlds. Walk through, and you're somewhere where the hamburgers eat people or the Nazis won the war or whatever. Your classic *Sliders*/ *Sliding Doors* scenario."

"Well, I don't know about the hamburgers, but the Nazi thing could happen," JD said after a moment, his tone revealing his annoyance. "If Hitler or FDR had been the person to walk through the doorframe, then maybe. Do you get it yet? The 'different world' isn't a location. The doorframe can't be programmed. There's no 'dial-up-this-universe' setting. The only thing you can actually 'set' on the controls is the time you spend in the alternate location. What the doorframe does is operate on the individual resonances of that particular observer."

He waited for me to interrupt him with more snark. When I didn't, he continued. "Okay, so here's how they described it to me. Instead of a metaphorical box with a metaphorical cat, think of a traffic light. A quantum traffic light, with three clear states: red, yellow, green. And then there's the driver and the road. All clear so far?"

"Crystal."

"Okay. So the driver in the car is the 'you,' or, more specifically, the 'quantum-observer.' When the car gets to the light, the light is *all the colors at once*. That's your quantum superposition: the unformed potentiality of existence. What the observer—the driver of the car—does, is either speeds up, slows down, or comes to a hard stop. When they make their choice—and remember, they make that choice the microsecond they see that light, the act of looking at that light itself is what makes that choice—the light changes. It becomes red, yellow, or green. All of a sudden the superposition collapses and the traffic light is just another traffic light, the road another road."

"The one paved with good intentions?"

"Ha." JD wasn't smiling. "No. Each direction, each traffic light, leads to what we would call a different reality, a different existence. A new road. So what that means in terms of the gate is simple: you walk through and you see a new road, the one that might have been, if you'd made another choice at the stoplight. That's why they nicknamed it the 'Might've Box.'"

"Bullshit," I said. "That doesn't make any sense. *Every* decision creates a new universe? Every second? And then those new universes branch off even further into exponentially larger ones? Infinite branching realities, all because someone chose to eat yogurt instead of a banana that morning?"

"You're right about the small decisions. Most of them have no real bearing on the nature of the universe," JD confirmed. "And neither do most people. The fact is, the majority spend their lives waiting on that yellow light, the destination never getting closer. They never decide whether to stop or go. They just wait. Their road never changes, their destination never wavers. They live a life without agency. And when this average yellow-light person walks through the doorframe, *nothing happens*. The typical person lived the life they were always meant to live, made the only choices and decisions that were possible for them to make, based on genes, environment, and circumstance. The complex stew of nature and nurture and chance that made them into a yellow-lighter. It turns out, free will is mostly an illusion and most people are living the exact life they were meant to live. The only life they ever could."

"But not you?" I asked.

"Not *us*," JD said. "And politicians, captains of industry, the majority of mothers, drone operators...the sort of jobs and lives that affect a lot of people. Also orthodontists, for some reason. An Air Force secretary had the record—something like 3000 recorded realities before she finally stopped returning."

The waitress came back, refilling our mostly-full cups and glancing pointedly at the check. The sky was starting to lighten outside the big windows, the stars beginning to fade. "You buying?" I asked.

JD smiled, took out his wallet and left two twenties for an $11 bill. "Any other questions?"

"I'm still not satisfied with the answers I've got," I replied. "You walk through this magic door—"

"The technical term for that 'walk' is a 'Liminal Externality Actualizing Process.'"

"L.E.A.P? Are you fucking kidding me? You do a goddamn *quantum leap*?"

JD hit me with a big old shit-eating grin and nodded. "I'm not fucking with you, but you've got to remember, these people are tremendous nerds. Honestly, coming up with that acronym is probably what gave me regular access to the gate. They're just maladjusted people, Jim. Easy to gull and easy to please."

"Oh yes, this mysterious 'they,'" I said after thinking through the implications. "But I still don't buy it. Where are 'they'? That's the big flaw in the theory right there. You're telling me if 'they' can do a 'leap' they wouldn't want to take that next step and do a grab? A steal?"

"There's the rub," JD said. "Travel is always one-way. Things can go from Universe A to Universe B, but the only things that can come back to Universe A are what came along in the first place." He paused for a second before pointing to the still mostly-full glass in front of him. "Do you have any idea what it feels like to have the half-digested food in your stomach and the water from your veins ripped out of your body? It's not great. I try not to eat too much when I'm here."

I winced.

JD nodded. "Yeah, it sucks. But it's probably a very good thing, if you think about it. If it wasn't for the one-way travel limit, we'd be invading and fracking every reality there was and sending all that oil back to Universe A."

"Is that the technical name?" I asked.

"Ha! No, there's no Universe A. I mean, there had to have been one somewhere, way way up the line. But the fact that in my universe—and probably yours—the Might've Box just appeared, means we're all subsidiary to whichever one first invented it."

"It's turtles all the way down," I said.

"Turtles all the way."

"So you walked through the door, did your quantum... I'm not calling it a *leap*."

"Amble," said JD. "Much more of a quantum amble."

That made me laugh for a second. "Alright, so the Pentagon liked you enough to give you access to, what, the subatomic pivot of all multiversal existence? As a perk for a visiting author?"

"It's all just people, Jim," JD said. "You'd be surprised how likable we can be when we want to. It's not all that hard to wear a mask, is it?"

"Okay, so you did your quantum amble, and then what?"

"It showed me what would have happened if I'd braked instead of accelerated at that quantum traffic light. I went through and found myself here...where I found my self... there." JD laughed again. "Gets a little confusing, doesn't it? Anyway, there's the twist, Jim. You're my road not taken."

My head started to spin. I considered the implications of what he was saying, that my whole life was just an uncollapsed quantum superposition, that I only existed because of the choices of an outside observer, that the existence of this *entire universe* was entirely dependent on the subjective actions of the person who broached the gate. The person sitting across the table from me.

"So what have you been up to this whole time? How did you find me?" I asked, at a loss for what else to say.

"It's called entanglement—our two selves, our two subjective realities, are inextricably linked. Whenever I arrive, I'm always within a ten minute walk or so from you. You were easy to find. And hell." JD looked pained. "It nearly broke my heart, seeing you like this. Seeing what might have been."

I had an abject urge to apologize before it soured. I felt a surge of rage at the audacity of this man and his pitying eyes, and had to collect myself before responding.

"Well, here we are," I finally said. "Now what?"

"Sun'll be up soon," JD replied. "Why don't we hit the road?"

CHAPTER THIRTEEN

We were on the highway again, desert dawn in the air. I drove carelessly and without aim. There was so much to take in; I needed time to reflect. JD's explanations had hit me like a semi truck, leaving me smeared and dazed across the roadscape of my mind.

I thought about JD and his picture-perfect writer's life, the improbable successes piling up. Fucking *Star Wars*. I could see him sitting in some plush Pentagon conference room, signing an NDA for his good friends in the Military Industrial Complex. I could see him walking into a secured area, wearing his familiar bantering mask. I knew just how he'd feign a casual cynicism at the discovery of this quantum bullshit, making the same jokes as I would about the evil mirror-universe from *Star Trek*. Did he hesitate when he approached the door for that first brief visit? Or did he not even consider the implications?

It felt goddamn presumptuous to be treated as a piece of science-fiction, to inhabit a universe that only exists because someone else existed.

Unless that other person only existed because of *my* choices.

That's what I kept focusing on. I was as real as the heartburn I felt, as real as the index cards in my shoebox, as real as anything in my life. I couldn't get a full grasp on the quantum implications of it all, the supposition of the resonances and all that bullshit. But I still remembered my Descartes: I thought, therefore I was...therefore, fuck you.

JD had waited patiently for us to get back on the interstate before speaking again. Finally, when the silence got too heavy, he asked me in a quiet voice: "What happened after high school, Jim?"

"Plenty," I answered.

"Plenty of what?"

"What kind of answers are you looking for, old sport? I got a GED. Time at a pissant community college. Mom and Dad died."

"Car crash?"

"Car crash."

"Do you ever think he killed her?"

"Sometimes." It was true, a truth I'd never spoken aloud. Dad did a very good job of driving drunk, always had. He'd never gotten a speeding ticket, let alone a DUI. He knew his business. I'd seen photos of the car wreck that had killed them both the summer after I'd left Reynolds, a stark image of a single car smashed into a single tree on an empty road. There were no skid marks on that road. No evidence of brakes.

It's a powerful thing, when your greatest doubt is confirmed aloud, to hear the echo of your suspicions.

I thought of crashing cars, of acceleration into the black. For a second— only a second—the car swerved on that desert highway.

"Yeah, I think he did. Miserable bastard," JD muttered. I made a murmur of agreement, thinking for a second about all the unpaid debts—real and metaphorical—Dad had left behind.

"How much did Dad's abuse fuck you up?" JD asked, breaking the silence.

The question stopped me short, made me want to pump the brakes. "Abuse? What do you mean?"

"Come on, you know. I know that you know. The rage? The violence? All the drinking? All those stays at rehab? You know." He gave a bitter laugh. "Dad stuff." His voice was light, but I felt the weight in it.

I kept my eyes on the road, thinking the question over. "Well, it was all a long time ago. I try not to let it bother me," I finally answered. "I've tried to move on."

JD's eyes looked at me with a pity that loomed large in my peripheral vision. "Have you ever heard of the ACES test?" he asked.

"The what?"

"Adverse Childhood Experience Survey. ACES. It's a clinical measure for quantifying childhood abuse."

"Abuse? Shit, man, is that what you think?" My reaction was instant. Reflexive. "Sure, Dad got mean when he drank, threw his fists around a bit. He was definitely an asshole. But child abuse? He never diddled us or anything. He was just a jerk."

JD was silent again for a moment, one stretching as long as the reach of that all-consuming desert darkness past the road's edge. A moment that stretched for a whole lifetime.

"Well, Jim, that's the power of the test," JD said at last. "It's what changed my life when I first heard about it. No one wants to have been an abused kid, do they, Jim? No one wants to hear that. But that's the power of the test. There's no room for bullshit. Just 'yes' or 'no.'"

"Well then my answer is, 'no,' I wasn't abused."

"Not that type of question, Jim. They're a lot more granular. The one I remember is, 'did a parent ever hit you so hard it left marks.' And the only answer we can give is 'yes.' Not 'well, he was just under a lot of pressure,' or 'I acted out as a kid, I baited him into doing it.' Just 'yes' or 'no.' And I know that answer, same as you."

"Is that it?"

"There's ten questions, Jim. Ten simple questions and a score. No ambiguity. Just a number."

"What's the damage?" I finally asked.

"With all the times he got drunk and violent, all the times he'd fly off into a rage and take a swing at us, we ended up with a score of five out of ten."

That didn't sound too bad to me. That didn't seem too bad at all. "Okay, fifty percent?" I asked. "That's workable, right? All things considered? Seems like it's pretty good."

JD gave a guttural laugh. "It works out to be about a 400% higher risk of depression and over a thousand percent higher risk of suicide than someone with a happy childhood."

I swallowed, hard. "That bad, huh."

"It sure as shit ain't good."

At least ten minutes passed in silence. They were hard ones. It felt like someone had crawled into the deepest and most primal core of my selfhood— that final shadowed, irreducible chamber—and turned on a wincingly bright light. In this shining and irresistible beam, all that was sacred and soft—everything that made up *me* and who I truly was —appeared as tawdry, sunbleached chintz.

I thought back to all those dark times in childhood, the times I was so afraid of this towering violent drunk, and for the first time I realized what it meant that, for so long, I had empathized not with the scared child, but with the brute. All at once I faced the truth I'd been running from my whole life.

None of the abuse was my fault. It had never been.

"So, what about the writing?" JD asked at last, and I felt my resentment swell. All of this, the turmoil, the violent reframing of my childhood, all of it, was because of him.

"What about it?" I said, after I mastered my breath.

"You told me you hadn't published anything since Reynolds, right?" I nodded.

"But you've kept writing, haven't you?"

"Yeah," I said. "I keep writing."

JD was silent for a moment. I took the exit off the interstate and onto the road that would take us to the malpaís. I didn't even realize that was where we were headed until I did it. But the location felt right somehow. Predestined.

"Has anyone else read what you've written since Reynolds?" JD asked.

"Yeah, I've had a few workshops," I admitted. "Some good feedback."

"In Los Angeles?"

"Yeah, Los Angeles." A thread of unease unspooled within my gut. We were moving past our shared past now, entering the place where my life had gone one way and his had gone another.

"With....?" I could feel JD looking at me.

"Some chick who worked at a coffee shop. That's all."

"Marcia Ibanez?"

"That's her."

"She's talented, isn't she?"

"She can definitely write. Shame that she ended up working on some sitcom instead of actually doing it, though." I was surprised by the bitterness in my voice. "Shame she sold out."

"Do you really consider what she did selling out?"

"I mean, if you've got talent and you waste it writing shitty jokes for a shitty show in a shitty medium, that strikes me as shitty."

"She's still writing though, isn't she?" JD said. "Selling something? Seems to me like it's better to be a sellout than something that never gets sold. What do they call that? Dead stock."

He was hitting home. I bit my tongue. My instinct was to lash out, to make him feel all the anger and disappointment that his words stirred up. I hated myself at that moment. I hated my selves.

I made a noncommittal noise and gathered my thoughts before responding. "So what, you breached the dimensional veil to give me a pep-talk about writing? I don't buy it. Why are you here, JD? Why are you really here?"

"That's fair. Alright, I can answer that. I'm going to tell you a little secret about life, Jimmy, as true for writing as anything else: success begets success. That's really all there is to it. You get one foot in the door and the rest comes easy. It all came so easy. One book gets published, and then your agent's doing all the work for you, you're signing bigger and bigger contracts. Next thing you know, you have all the editors and researchers and interns you could ever want. A whole team devoted to the singular purpose of making each book the best it could ever be." He pulled out his smartphone, the little screen illuminating my peripheral, and began to tap with his thumb.

"I've got 10 published books and four original shooting scripts on this thing, and some of the writing...I feel like I barely recognize it. It's been through so many revisions." JD had worked himself up. There was a thready desperation in his voice that was familiar and grating: the sound of self-pity. "And I know a lot of it is bullshit. I mean, with *Star Wars*, it was so easy. How do you fuck up *Star Wars*? The project fell right into my lap and all I had to do was some basic script doctoring. I gave the nerds what they wanted, added some simple Jungian archetypes, a few call-backs, subverted some expectations and fulfilled others. So easy. Took me two weeks to punch-up a script that made two billion dollars. It was just *too* easy, Jim."

JD continued. "Once I'd had a hit, then everything afterwards fell right into place. I started to doubt myself. Started to doubt whether or not the talent I'd thought I had was ever real or if it was all just luck, combined with the head start of being a straight white male." He caught himself, paused, and then resumed in a much more controlled voice. "I had a real bad case of impostor syndrome, you know? The sense that the successes came too easy to ever mean anything real." He gave a laugh, which felt forced. "I was starting to drift a bit, I guess. Trouble focusing on the work, spending too much time looking inward. Wondering if any of it was deserved, wondering if I'd spent all my talent in my twenties and was just coasting on the fumes." He stopped speaking right as we pulled into the turn off to the lot at the visitor center. "Where are we?" he asked.

"The bad land," I answered.

JD laughed. "Been there," he said.

CHAPTER FOURTEEN

The dawn had begun in earnest, the sky turning pale. We sat in the front seat of the idling car, the heat on high. It gets cold in the desert.

"So you were hitting a rut," I said, my voice shaded with sarcasm. "Full of impostor syndrome. Things just came too easy for you, all your success and validation turning hollow." His rant over how hard it was to be successful soured in my stomach like a gas-station burrito, still frozen in the middle. "So what?"

"Then came DARPA, Jim, and it was perfect. I had the opportunity to answer my questions, the existential ones that can tear a man up otherwise," JD said. "Was my success luck or skill? Had I made the right decisions in life? Did I have talent or just a lucky hand?"

"The player or the play," I said.

"Exactly. See, from what I can tell, that's the big twist. That's the big branch in our lives. We both went to Reynolds, both got caught copying that stupid capstone. We both ended up back home, getting our GED. Our parents died when we were 19. Everything was just the same, until one day it wasn't."

"So what happened?" I said, my heart pounding. I didn't want to know. I wanted to know more than anything. I wanted both, the either and the or.

"When was the last time you failed at something? Really failed?" JD asked.

I had to think about it. My first instinct was a kind of cynical despair, to point to the failure evident in the ruination I'd made of my life. But then I really considered the question. Up until this evening I'd been, if not a successful casino dealer, certainly not a failure of one. Beyond that, I assiduously avoided debts. I hadn't made an enemy in years, kept my nose clean and minded my business. I had a decent bank account, no insurmountable health problems, even something like a friendship with the Judsons and a couple of the croupiers down at the Deuces. These weren't high-class sophisticates—certainly no salons— but they were good people.

Finally I came back to the dreams I'd always had, the frustrated ones that seemed more and more impossible with each passing year. The dream of being a writer, of living up to all my potential. "It's obvious, isn't it?" I asked JD. "Of course I'm a failure. I'm not you, am I? I'm not the bigshot script doctor or novelist. I'm just me, another dim and anonymous sad sack."

"And you wanted to be me, didn't you? Really wanted it?" JD was staring at me in a way that made me feel uncomfortable, that made me want to avert my eyes.

"Of course I did. I still do," I said, resigned.

"But you never...what?"

"Oh, fuck you," I answered, my voice a guttural growl. "Quit your leading questions. What are you trying to say? That you worked harder after high school and I didn't? I've worked hard every goddamn day of my life."

JD was nodding his head eagerly. "Of course it's not working harder, Jim. I wouldn't bullshit you with something so trite. But the answer is plain. You've got all these ideas—multimillion dollar ones— but they've never left your shoebox. You spend all day high on the fumes of your own self-regard, your ego. And the source of that ego is obvious. When you think of yourself, when you picture who you really are, it's not 'James Dougherty: middle-aged aspiring writer.' It's as that Reynolds kid, isn't it? You in junior year, the height of our powers? The clever smartass with all that unformed potential just waiting to come out?"

I nodded back. All my sharp rejoinders died in the dryness of my throat. He was right.

"It's a powerful feeling!" JD said, his voice rising like a preacher. The bastard was really enjoying himself. "To be young and full of potential. It's like you're almost buoyant, like you're riding on a big floating balloon just full of the most powerful substance there is: potential. You could be anything, be anyone. It's so easy to float high above the petty vagaries of the day-to-day, to keep yourself removed from those downlow annoyances and necessities, the heartbreaks and setbacks. You're going places, feeling full and high above the rest of them. It's easy and safe up there in the clouds. Just drifting. Because that's the other side to that potential, Jim. It can keep you afloat for a real long time, but it sure can't steer your course. And that balloon is always leaking as you age, too, deflating slow and steady. There's nothing sadder than a sagging balloon, is there, Jim?"

I thought of my empty days of half-life watching bad TV and reading airport thrillers, the long nights working a dead-end job in a dead-end town. Alone except for the nagging call of all that I'd abandoned, those opportunities I never pursued, the people I never let get too close. There wasn't anybody coming after me, hoping to track me down. Opportunity had knocked and I'd kept the door locked. The only ones still looking for me were my regrets.

I nodded again.

JD gave me a smile, a real one, full of understanding. I felt something inside me break a little.

"I remember my first failures perfectly, Jim," he said. "I treasure them. All those rejected pitches, all the drafts sent back torn to shreds with red lines and excisions, the articles that just came back with a single 'no' on them. You want to know the truth, Jim? The secret ingredient to success? It's *failure*. You've lived so long with that self-perception, you've spent so long up in the clouds, you're afraid of the alternative. You know that if you try your best, actually do the work, and don't get instant success? That validation? Then it was all a lie. You're not that kid anymore. A rejection will shatter those illusions like nothing else."

"And you know what?" JD continued. "It will. But that's okay. Who'd want to spend their life stuck in a permanent adolescence on some Holden Caulfield trip? My balloon popped long ago. It popped the second I volunteered for the newspaper at the community college and had an editorial rejected for being 'glib and slapdash.' I still remember that feeling, how angry I got at the editor. How my first instinct was to tell her 'fuck off,' secure in the knowledge that I was a genius and she was just some twat at a community college."

We both paused to watch the distinctive sleek shape of a roadrunner bobbing its head as it moseyed in front of the car, taking its time as it wandered about on its unaccountable journey, going from here to there upon the earth.

"Well would you look at that?" JD said, his voice soft with wonder. "I've got to get out to the desert more often." The bird sauntered onwards and we both sat silently for a moment before JD continued, speaking in a tender tone.

"The only thing that can truly convert potential is effort, Jim. And that means trying. That means leaving the comfort of your self-image and seeing yourself for who you really are. You can't get there from the clouds. You got to get real low with it, no illusions. You've got to pop your balloon and take that hard fall. And then you gotta get back up again. And before you know it, you'll be making progress. You'll be walking on your own two feet, leaving that empty balloon behind you. You'll realize that the thing holding you up your whole life, the thing that kept you safe and isolated and high above the rest, was nothing. Just barely a promise. A bunch of hot air."

"So what? You're saying that because you embraced your identity as a failure, you somehow became successful? Some kind of paradox?"

"Not at all, Jim. I never thought I was a failure. I just realized it was *okay* to fail. It was actually a good thing, because that's how you get better. I realized there was more to me than 'gifted kid,' and that I'd just been making excuses as to why I never tried—telling myself I believed in the dream of the tortured genius, the evoker of the muse. I had two very real and very damaging ideas at the heart of my self-perception: that I was still that Reynolds kid inside, full of unformed brilliance, and that I just had to wait long enough and the world would recognize it. I had been telling myself—lying to myself— for so long, saying the perfect moment would come, that perfect moment to write: that moment when the combination of inspiration and experiences and talent might alchemize into that perfect afflatus—a divine spark—after which the perfect story and the perfect life would just happen."

He waited for me to speak. I didn't, just kept my eyes locked on the patch of sage where the roadrunner had disappeared. I was waiting for the coyote.

When the silence got too weighted, JD continued. "That was what I learned at the community college, what I learned at the alt-weekly I interned at afterwards, the two years after that I spent as a hapless freelancer. I learned that sure, I had potential. I could string together a couple of sentences real fine. I had my shoebox and its index cards. But it all added up to nothing, absolutely nothing, compared to finishing something on my own. I realized that I learned quite a bit; probably got more practical skills from the 'community college twat' than I ever did in an AP English class. I ended up sending her a check when I sold my first book."

His voice changed to somber. "I get it Jim, I really really do." I felt the heft of his gaze on the side of my face and forced myself to keep looking at the empty patch of desert. "I understand the feeling better than anyone, the tantalizing promise of 'your someday,' the lift of that balloon. But that vision is a liar, Jim, the one that tells you to keep waiting. Because you wait long enough, and time will take everything away from you. Everything you'd ever had and anything you might ever want."

My chest pounded and my veins throbbed. My jaw clenched as I forced myself to meet his gaze, his face (*my face!)* open and beseeching. He was right. The bastard was right. And I knew it. I'd wasted my entire life waiting for someone else to do the hard work of transforming an idea on an index card into a novel, into a script, into something besides an idea with a lot of potential. That someone was the future me. And, with a certainty that tasted like copper in my mouth, I realized the future me would never come. I could waste my whole life waiting. I already had.

In that instant, a fully-formed vision popped into my head. It was of the Judsons, sitting in their parking lot and sipping lemonade while their children played in the twilight. They weren't alone, though. I sat right beside them, along with a barely sketched in Mormon bride (sturdy, buxom) and a few towheaded kids of our own.

Here was a "someday" right in front of me, a good life I could have, that I'd already earned. It wouldn't be glamorous, it wouldn't be in answer to some nebulous calling or unfulfilled potential, no muse, no "life I was always meant to live." But it would be good. And it would be all mine. My branch. One where I'd already paid my dues.

JD was continuing to speak, self-absorbed as ever. The coolness of that domestic vision faded, and I was left with the rage I felt towards the person sitting next to me. That rage began to crystalize into a diamond-hard determination and a plan.

"There's not some big secret, some lightning flash of inspiration after which everything just pours out fully formed. Brewster Bradley was right about everything," JD droned on, repeating himself now. "There are no easy ways out. It's just hard work. The hard work of revising, editing, re-writing, pitching, and writing again. There's no shortcut to hard work. I spent my twenties doing it."

I thought of my lost years, the few hungover mornings I could remember. Those 2:00 PM mornings, rolling bloated out of my sheetless bed or beer-soaked couch, my nose clogged with bleach-scented coke, and no one to turn to but a trashcan full of vomit. There are whole years full of petty deals and half-assed schemes that I can barely remember. I'd been living, damn it, trying to be that *enfant terrible*, the melange of Brett Easton Ellis, Hunter S. Thompson, Hemingway, Kerouac, and Bukowski. I thought I'd been laying the groundwork, getting a start. But all the while, that asshole JD was plugging away on the campus mimeograph, lapping me before I'd even begun to run.

And then after that, the arc of my life: getting sober(ish), finding regular employment as a barista. Maybe that should have been my starting point, when Marcia and I had exchanged our writing, when my head was a little clearer.

The thought of Marcia stopped me cold.

"Wait a second." I interrupted JD's self-righteous monologue. "You mentioned Marcia Ibanez earlier. But I didn't meet her until I was in my thirties. How could you have known her?"

"She's the love of your life, Jim," JD said, after a wistful pause. "The love of our lives. She's my whole world."

"But... we were both working at the Double Shot when we met, during the time you were supposedly on the easy path to success. That doesn't make sense," I protested. "Where did you meet her?"

"At the same coffee shop you did, back when I had a condo in Santa Monica. I used to write there when she worked there. We got to talking. She's so sharp, so funny. We started collaborating—first *Auld Acquaintances*—and then one of those stupid sitcoms, and then on love." JD gave a chuckle. "Remember what I said about free will being mostly an illusion? Some things are just meant to be." He threw open the car door. "Let's go for a walk."

The air was bracing. I took a few deep breaths, watched the last of the nightjars flock in the rising light. I went to the trunk of my car and opened it. Inside were the things I'd spent the last month preparing, all neatly packed away.

Before me were the fruits of my doppelgänger research. I had a little bottle full of holy water and a consecrated Bible and rosary I'd purchased at the Las Vegas Diocese, intended as a defense against a fetch. Next to them were five different paintings of my favorite foods— printed out images of burgers and pizza I'd traced over with acrylic paint—intended to bind or confuse a Ka. These were worthless. But they weren't the only things I had brought.

Next to them was a backpack, a bag I'd found in my storage unit when I'd gone to find Mom's cookie recipe. Inside that bag were some snacks, carefully labeled, a big bottle of water, and a floppy hat. I'd learned from the last time I'd come out here; I wouldn't disrespect the sun. I took the bag out and stretched, pasting a smile on my face which I hoped looked real. The grimace on JD's face when he saw mine told me that it didn't.

"Hey, I know all that was a lot to take on," he said gently. "But now we're on the same page, right? You know why I'm here, where we're different. I know it wasn't luck—we have the same ideas—but really just hard work and a little change in mindset that made me successful." That self-righteous fuck was trying not to sound triumphant. "And now I can help you out, right? There's no reason why not. Let's start with the obvious: why haven't you finished a story?"

"Haven't found the time," I muttered.

JD just looked at me. "The time?" he questioned. "You've got no girlfriend, no dependents, no expensive addictions. You work—worked—a decent job, and live in a $500 a month rental. Seems to me you've got plenty of money and plenty of time."

I felt the arrows striking home. He was right. It was just an excuse. I had plenty of free time, no pressing obligations or debt. There was nothing standing in the way of my success but me. I'd spent so long blaming everyone I could—from capitalism and this broken country's broken culture, all the way to the ineffable lack of a muse—that I couldn't see the obvious. It was me. I was still my own worst enemy. I always would be.

"Yeah, alright. That was tough love, huh?" I asked him. "Now we move on to the pep talk?"

"Jim, I know you too well for that." He pointed east. "It's time for the sunrise."

CHAPTER FIFTEEN

We marched along the narrow trail to Rabbit Ear Lookout, the same one I'd climbed a month ago. I felt numb, the ringing kind that comes in the wake of an explosion. My eyes were locked on the path ahead. JD was nearly vibrating with his good cheer; he seemed downright chipper. And why not? He'd had his moment, his catharsis and his answers. He'd heard what he wanted to hear: that he deserved his good fortune. He kept whistling the same song, the chorus to Carly Simon's "You're So Vain." It was our mother's favorite tune.

The sun rose at last in triumph, great lances of pink and gold stabbing across the sky. JD stopped and pointed to the distance where a pair of coyotes slunk across a distant lava ridge.

"So what's next?" he asked me. "I'll be able to come back in a few weeks. I'd love to take a look at whatever you've got written then." He laughed to himself. "Get another set of eyes on it, right?"

"Maybe. I've got a lot to think about," I said, sullen. I stared at the man—his expensive and stylish clothes only lightly dampened with sweat, the assurance that can only come from consistent success and the posture that comes from being at ease—and felt a deep abiding hatred at his presumption.

I thought about the ways I hadn't known him at first, hadn't wanted to see what was right in front of my eyes. It was the same with everything in my life, every mistake and regret and unfulfilled urge. Not seeing JD came from the same mental defense mechanism that had kept me from seeing the obvious: I was the source of all my problems.

I felt that split again. Everything about JD seemed so clear and obvious, like he was the real person and me the distorted reflection from some rundown dust-streaked funhouse mirror. The weight of that clarity kept me stooped.

We arrived at the bench and took in the sunrise. The way the rosy gauze of dawn contrasted with the harsh black of the lava-flow was remarkable, like a great malignant watermelon wedge placed atop a rocky, barren sea.

"What came first," I finally asked, "the success or the confidence? Were you confident because of your successes, or successful because of your confidence?"

JD gave me a pitying look. "The writing came first, Jim. Always. I wrote, and felt terrible about what I wrote, but I kept at it. I had editors tell me it was trite, self-absorbed, and rambling, but I kept at it. I got so many rejections, but just kept at it. And, after a while, I did get confidence in myself and my abilities. They weren't all rejections. I started to take pride in my successes and learn from the failures. And, before too long, I just started feeling *right*. Like I was doing what I was supposed to be doing. It all came easy after that. Just like it was meant to be."

I had nothing to say. I felt broken, beaten by the buffeting force of his words, the knowledge that there actually was a right way to do things, a universally approved path, that I'd ignored. In the great game of life, JD had rounded the board while I'd been stuck on start. He was the winner and I the loser—cosmically, metaphysically. On every level.

"Was it really that easy?" I said. "All I had to do was *try?*"

"Of course not, Jimmy. Success took a lot of luck, I'll admit it. And I had to overcome some demons, same as you. But what I think it really all came down to was fear. You're too afraid to try, but maybe it's not just because you were scared to fail. Maybe you were really just scared because you were already so afraid..."

"Afraid of what?"

"Jim, don't put up a front. We had the same childhood. We have the same memories. You know what Dad did to us, the kind of shit he did to a little kid. He wasn't just an asshole. He was the type of drunk who beat the shit out of a seven year old. The type of drunk who makes that kid believe they deserved it."

I started to tremble a little, my hands shaking with adrenaline. I stayed silent until I couldn't, until I said "Well, I guess you got over it then," in a small and bitter voice.

"I never got over it, Jim. How could we?" He shook his head and paused before continuing. "But I'm grateful, I'm so grateful, that I learned I had something I needed to get over. When I took that test, I learned that what had happened was undeniable. That my—our—

abuse was as plain as any score. That's when I learned I had a problem. And that was the true start."

"Of the writing?"

"Of everything!" He spread his hands wide, encompassing that all. "Once I realized how much of me, how much of *us*, was just a facade, an elaborate front...a mask. Once I realized that, well it got me thinking about what I was hiding or, really, what I was protecting. It was that little kid, Jim. All of it—the desire to keep other people far away or as an audience instead of as peers, the easily punctured and untested arrogance which kept me high above all the rest, the constant strain between wanting to succeed and the fear of actually being seen —all of it. Every part. It was all just trying to protect that little kid, the one who had to wear long-sleeve shirts all springtime in second grade because he had to hide the bruises. Just trying to keep that little kid safe."

I nodded, silent tears rolling down my face.

"It's okay, Jim. I understand. I understand it so well. I know how scared that wincing little kid is. Of not living up to his potential. Of rejection. Of never, ever getting his 'someday.' I understand where it comes from, that fear. You're avoiding those answers, you don't want to know if your potential was real or fake, so you never tried. You didn't want to get hurt, so you never really lived."

His words were kind, but his tone was smug and self-satisfied, like someone explaining the second-act twist or an English professor pointing out the meaning of the green light on the far dock. The obvious pleasure he was taking in having figured me out dried my tears, replacing them with a tightened throat and reddened cheeks. Anger replacing regret.

It seemed like a life of success had given JD a lot of self-reflection and considerable inner growth.

It made me think about what else he had that I didn't.

"Tell me more about Marcia," I finally asked, once my emotions were under control.

JD gave me a long look. "Are you sure you want to hear about her?"

I nodded, and he continued.

"She's magic, Jim, she really is. I know 'soulmate' sounds hack, but there's no other word for her. Hell, the fact that we both knew her confirms it." His face broke into a big smile. "It really was meant to be," he repeated himself, his voice muted. "It was all just meant to be."

I stared at his face the whole time, watched it move through wistfulness into real satisfaction and contentment, watched his smile as he confirmed for himself once more that everything was coming up roses for ol' JD. I don't think he saw me see him, though.

JD caught himself. I watched the features melt, the mask come on. "And don't you worry, Jim," he said earnestly. "I'm sure it'll happen for you two as well. We'll get those stories published, get you an agent. Then you can go look her up. It'll happen for you, same as for me." He gave me the most earnest and guileless expression we had.

And in that moment, I knew. He was bullshitting me, putting on the same false mask I knew all too well, familiar from the daily bullshit at the tables and laying on the corn for the Judsons. It was a liar's face. And it took one to know it.

I thought about that look, the earnest falsehood hiding his genuine contentment, his pleasure at this whole interdimensional excursion. JD's story was done. He'd had his catharsis, his hero's journey. I didn't fit into this JD's life, not really. I sat with the knowledge that, at best, I might get a couple more visits from the man, a few pieces of hollow encouragement to keep up the hard work. Then one day, nothing. I'd be left with nothing but the heavy truth that I could've been someone but wasn't.

He could do it, easy. He could turn his back on his past and just keep moving forward, secure in the knowledge that he'd made the right choices, done the right things. I knew, better than anyone, how simple it would be.

In that instant, I decided.

I sat down on the bench and unpacked the bag I'd brought. Inside was a thermos, a stale PB-and-J, and two batches of cookies, wrapped up in tin foil and kept in separate plastic bags. I took a long swallow of lukewarm water and passed it over to JD, who took a smaller one.

A wave of loneliness washed over me, both a promise and a premonition. I'd spent so long alone, placated by the certainty that it would all be worth it, someday. There'd only been a few women over the past year, bar assignations and one-night-stands, that never outlasted the morning. And all the while, JD was celebrating his success in the arms of his (*my!*) soulmate.

I unwrapped my cookies.

"So here's what we're going to do," JD continued, his expression as innocent and open as a grave. "You're going to get to work on your *Time and Tide* story about the lifeboat. That's a good idea, it's one I've never had before. It's got juice, real *potential.*" He stopped and gave me a wink.

I started to eat.

"So then I'm going to drop back in, maybe in a couple weeks from now. Oh, maybe a month, I forgot about Cannes. But I'll come back, and we're going to work on some edits. I'll hook you up with your version of my agent, my manager. Help you write a pitch letter. We're going to get you started off on the right foot. And then—hey, are those Mom's cookies?"

They were. In a way.

I'd been thinking of the cookies ever since JD's first visit. I'd gone looking for the recipe in my storage unit and found it in the little rubbermaid that carried all that remained of my mother's life. Her entire legacy. I'd made a half-dozen batches before I was satisfied with the results, but I'd finally done it.

"They are," I told JD, handing him the other package of cookies out of my backpack. I had been methodically working my way through mine while JD buzzed on with his pep-talk bullshit.

JD unwrapped his package, took out a cookie and stared at it for a moment. He looked me in the eyes. "Where did you find the recipe?"

"It was with the rest of Mom's stuff. Didn't you ever go through it?"

JD's eyes narrowed in a quick spasm of guilt. "Ah, well. I meant to. Still do. But, well. You know. Things get misplaced." He looked back at the cookies. "I'm going to pay for this later on, but fuck it. It's not every day you get to eat your dead mom's cookies alongside your doppelgänger." He gave me a theatrical wink. "Sometimes you just have to go with the moment; sometimes the moment arrives."

He took a big bite and began to chew. He smiled. "God, they're good. So fucking good. Just like Mom used to make. Just like those old days." He closed his eyes for a moment's reverie and continued to speak. "We're going to make this happen for you, James! We really are. You're going to get the book, get the agent, the girl and the life. And all you have to do is get to work."

I recognized what JD was doing now. He was playing for an audience. Performing his great and generous act of absolution, performing the climax to whatever story he thought he was living.

He forgot that I had a story as well.

"You're going to succeed, my man!" JD continued, pumping his fist like a mad desert prophet. "And the key to that success is the struggle. It'll be so much sweeter after having worked for it. You'll get the deep satisfaction that comes from self-actualization, that comes from knowing that you did what you had to do. From doing the work. It's all about that work, right? 'Chop wood, carry water,' and all that shit? I wouldn't want to cheat you out of that with any shortcuts. You know, in some ways, I'm jealous. You're going to get to do it all over again. Learn you really do have what it takes."

With his eyes fixed on the horizon, at an audience that wasn't really there out on the lava, JD never saw my glare. He never saw how the condescension in his tone made me want to hit him, or that I could see how false it all was, just empty bullshit and fake promises. He turned his gaze to me and I darted mine back to the desert panorama in front of us. I put on my mask, gave him a big smile back. "Well hell, JD!" I said. "Sounds like things are going to work out just fine for me. I owe you a lot."

JD's eyes narrowed a bit. I'm sure he sensed the sarcasm, but I kept my face as earnest as his. He just nodded back.

We sat side by side in tense and empty quiet for a while, watching the sun rise in the sky. We ate our dead mom's cookies and watched the clouds burn away. We talked for a bit, about Mom and about Dad, and then reverted back to silence.

Finally, JD began to sneeze. Again and again. And again. He rubbed his face, rubbed his eyes. His nose was running something fierce. "Ah, this goddamn hayfever!" he said, his voice a gargle. "Did you take a Claritin or something?" He rubbed his eyes until his knuckles turned white.

I knew that it was time.

"No, I didn't take a Claritin, JD. But I still have a question. What I really want to know, JD, the one thing you've never answered to my satisfaction, is where did you get the fucking nerve?" I growled.

JD coughed, cleared his throat, spat. He rubbed his eyes before answering. "Excuse me?"

"I'm just dying to know. I mean, this is a pretty big decision you made here. According to you, your presence here fixed the states, maybe even created this entire universe. All because of you and your curiosity. And you had the nerve to talk to me about *my ego?*"

"I don't understand," JD wheezed.

"I'm sure you don't. I mean, your big motive was what, upper class malaise? The magnitude of your success causing you impostor syndrome? Did you really breach the fucking interdimensional veil on a journey of *self-discovery?* Well, here's the self you discovered, asshole.

Me. I'm not a metaphor, I'm not the goddamn Goofus to your Gallant, your cautionary tale. I'm every bit as real as you. Sure, I wasn't some big-shot Hollywood prick, never got around to finishing that book, let alone a string of bestsellers. But I still could've, I really could. But now I never will, not really. You stole my 'someday.' You stole my second act."

The sickly man had the grace to look abashed, feeling the weight of my words. He kept rubbing his eyes as started to speak. "Jimmy—Jim —I'm sorry, I truly am. I know I didn't handle this right at all, I know it was a little theatrical. I'm sorry." He rubbed his throat now, his voice coming out scratchy. "And yeah, I guess I didn't really consider the quantum possibilities of it all."

"I mean, what's to consider?" I asked. "Just an entire universe. An entire life."

JD looked pained. His eyes were starting to goggle a bit. I think he started to suspect. "I'm, I'm sorry," he said. "But I'm genuine. I really am. I really do want to help you." He broke off, coughing, hawking up a wad of spit and giving an asthmatic whine. "Because I love you, Jim. I love you more than anyone. I love you."

"Well that's the fucking twist then—that's our difference," I spat. "Because me? I can't stand myself."

JD's eyes widened.

He knew.

I smiled.

"Low self-esteem, is that the root of my problems?" I asked, enjoying myselves. "A compulsion towards self-destruction?" I leaned in close and whispered, "Or is it the simple and undeniable fact that I am my own worst enemy?"

"I can't, I can't..." JD gasped.

"Can't what? Can't breathe?"

I picked up the tin foil wrapper of cookies that had fallen off his lap. "I don't think you're all that much smarter than me, JD. I mean, you've clearly been luckier, seem to have gotten whatever kick-in-the-ass I never did, the one that kept you writing. But I really don't think you're that much smarter. In fact, there's only one thing I'm certain that you know and I don't."

JD bent over, his head between his knees. His breath came in tortured whoops. I held up the cookies. "The one thing for sure that you know and that I don't, is what a real macadamia muncher tastes like, the kind Stacy Ketterling's mom used to make. I did always wonder if they were better than Mom's hazelnut ones, y'know? Was the grass greener?" I gave them a shake. "The ones I ate were Mom's recipe. They hold up. But were the other ones better? I guess I'll never know."

JD didn't answer.

Anaphylaxis is a slow and subtle process that unfolds in various ways. It can take anywhere from a couple minutes to several hours after the ingestion of the allergen before the onset of symptoms. What gets you isn't the substance itself, but your own body. Your own immune system starts to overreact, to poison itself, and becomes its own worst enemy. When those symptoms begin, they come on rapidly and require immediate intervention.

JD had eaten one-and-a-half cookies. When I made them (using rubber gloves and a face respirator) I'd been very careful. I used hazelnuts and followed mom's recipe precisely. But I'd made a couple substitutions, grinding up a dozen macadamia nuts and adding them to the flour, then supplementing the butter with macadamia oil I'd bought at the health food store in Vegas.

I'd made the cookies as part of my Ka/clone/Fetch trunk defense kit. The paintings and the holy water had proven worthless, and I'd learned that JD wasn't a clone. But those cookies sure did end up coming in handy.

JD's death was slow. And painful. He scratched at his throat and pissed his pants, clawed at his swollen eyes. I turned my back and watched the day's raw unveiling.

After the first seizure I felt his hand upon my leg. I faced him, looking down. It was too late and we both knew it. His grotesquely swollen face had blinded him. His breath was painful gasps. He looked for me. He reached out that hand yet again. I didn't take it.

I let him die alone.

Once it was over, after that final rattle, I dragged the body away from the bench and off the trail, into the frozen lava of the Malpais. I pushed him below a little protruding ridge that was a few minutes away. You couldn't see it from the bench.

After another hour JD's phone started to beep in my hand. The alarm was going off. I walked back to the little ridge where I found nothing but a puddle and a small pile of chewed-up, semi-digested cookies. I left those for the birds.

Before I walked back to my car, I sat at that bench, between the two tall pillars of Rabbit Ear Lookout. I looked through JD's phone. My thumbprint unlocked it, same as his.

There was a bit of a learning curve with clicking on all the stupid icons, figuring out how it all worked. But there, on the first screen, I saw one "app" called "Books" that, when clicked on, showed me tiny thumbnail sized copies of everything JD had ever published.

When I clicked on them, they blew up to full-screen size, cover and all. There were those ten completed novels, many of which had bestseller status printed on the covers of their newest edition. A couple had the "Major Motion Picture Coming Soon!" banner across the top.

The script PDFs were in there too, the shooting versions that had gone through the full process of revisions and had transparent DO NOT DUPLICATE watermarks on the page.

I had everything he did. My entire life's work.

I drove back home, sunburnt and giddy. The Judsons were doing chores out front, as usual. Ma had been joined by some frumpy twenty-something in long shorts and a four-year-old running around. They waved me over but I had other things on my mind. I just waved back, unlocked my door and went inside.

That night, I didn't dream a thing.

CHAPTER SIXTEEN

I'm sure you saw *Silicon Daddy*. Who didn't? The thing was a massive hit. All four-quadrants! We've got two sequels lined up. We decided to soften the ending just a tad, leaving it a little more open-ended and a little less grim. It really seemed to work out well.

Those of you in The Industry would call it absurd, the ease with which a thirty-something guy could come out of nowhere with nothing but a bunch of pilfered PDFs and end up with agents, production deals, contracts and first-looks and ridiculous advances. And, of course, you're right. It is in fact absurd. But that's the world, right? Absurd. What Camus called the product of the "confrontation between the human need and the unreasonable silence of the world."

I was just fortunate that, in my case, the world talked back. Gave me what I needed. What I took.

It was all so easy. All I had to do was take that first step and the rest fell right into place, all the threads of *'meant-to-be'* and *'almost-was'* fastened tight around me. Cold pitches were met with warm receptions. All the people who'd known JD in his other life were missing me; they just hadn't known it. Yet.

I looked up JD's agent and found that agent's assistant. I sent them the same pitch JD had used to sell *Fermi's Echo*. That was enough to get them interested in taking a look at the draft.

JD'd been right about one thing: all those editors really did make the work much better. Rereading one of JD's books was unnerving. I kept hearing the phantom echo of his keyboard the whole time, kept sensing his mind (my mind, our mind) at work upon the page. It was so familiar, yet all so strange. But there, embarking upon the winding trail of our words, I could see the hands of others, the ideas that would never have occurred to me, and I trusted them.

Once I had an agent, I just kept moving forward. *Fermi's Echo* was a respectable debut and critically acclaimed, enough to ensure that my script treatments got looked at. I had a few offers, which I declined. Instead, I approached JD's old rep and showed him the script for *Silicon Daddy*. That was enough. The universe kept working in my favor.

Between *Silicon Daddy* and *Fermi's Echo* I was a hot commodity. I got an enormous advance on *Quoth the Raven*, enough for me to send the Judsons 50 grand. They deserved that much at least. They didn't know what might have been.

Brewster Bradley sent me a letter after *Quoth the Raven*. It was weird. There wasn't much to it, just a "how ya been, remember when" type thing, almost too studied in its casualness. A quick Google showed me how Brewster had really stagnated; he was still teaching at Reynolds without much to show for the intervening years beyond a potbelly and a bald spot. At first, I considered lots of responses. After all, JD's edition of *Quoth the Raven* was dedicated "To Brewster Bradley: who showed me I had something to say for myself," but I hadn't dedicated mine. I kept my edition blank.

I didn't answer Brewster's letter. I've got no time for that high school shit. I've moved on.

Within a couple years of JD's death, I was on top of the world. I was making real money and a real name for myself. My agents love me, I hand in publishable material every six months like clockwork. Just like he said: it's easy.

After that start, Marcia came next. I'd printed out a few of the emails Marcia and JD had exchanged when they started dating. I sent her a letter, using some of the other Marcia's old phrases, which really seemed to resonate. She remembered me from the coffee shop. I played it cool.

After we'd been talking for a couple weeks I sent her a few pages of *Auld Acquaintances*, the ones that had the most sense of her in them; the saddest, loveliest and most heartbreaking sections. I told her I'd written them while thinking of her.

All I needed was that first step and I felt the universe shift. She fell in love with me reading her own words and didn't even know it. Marcia told me that I had written the sentences she'd always wanted to write, but never could. She told me reading them was like finding the other half of her soul. For me, it felt like finding the other half of my world.

Well, one thing led to another after that. Between our two careers we could afford somewhere real nice up in the Palisades, up in the hills with a view of the ocean and the desert at my back. It feels right. I've even taken up sailing. I keep a little sailboat down at the marina. Just the one though. And I never drive it back against the current; I beat on, real smooth.

♠♥♣♦

Was that the happy ending you expected? I got the career, got the girl, got the *meaning*. I have everything I've ever wanted, everything that was ever meant for me. It seems like a natural ending point. But it's not the ending; there never is one, besides the grave. There's still a complication. Of course there's still a twist. Those are the rules, right? No good deed goes unpunished.

I wake up early most days. There's just so much to do. I do my morning meditations, my affirmations and my exercises, all usually before dawn. Sometimes it's hard to sleep. There are times when I think of the restful oblivion I used to get down at the Gem-And-I with real jealousy.

On this particular morning—just a few weeks ago—I padded downstairs as the sun broke wide and forgiving over the horizon of the distant ocean. I took a moment to enjoy the view through the big picture windows in the living room. Life's too short, you know? You have to make time to enjoy it.

When I walked into the kitchen for my morning coffee, Juana was agitated. I like her to come in the early mornings; it's nice to wake up to a fresh breakfast and a running laundry machine and a smile from a grateful maid. But Juana clearly had a lot on her mind, her eyes darting back and forth to me and the front door and the staircase. I asked what was the matter. She hesitated for a moment, then confessed her concern over Marcia.

When Juana arrived at work this morning, the streets were dark and nearly empty. As she pulled up to the electronic gate, Marcia was waiting in the dark. According to Juana, Marcia hadn't seemed like herself at all, but had instead been awfully strange and jumpy. She said she'd lost her key, so Juana let her in.

I could tell Juana had questions, but it wasn't her place to ask them. I didn't relieve her curiosity, merely thanked her for loyalty and discretion. I told her that I was going to wait for my breakfast and for her to keep it warm.

I went back upstairs to the bedroom where Marcia—*my* Marcia— was still snoring softly. She's a very heavy sleeper and rarely gets up before nine. I left her sleeping and began to search the house.

It didn't take very long. My study—the place where I don't write— is kept clean and pristine. It's decorated plainly, the bookshelves full of the first editions I can now afford. I've still got the same black walnut writing desk, even still have the box of index cards. Everything was just as I'd left it but the desk wasn't empty. There was a slim manilla envelope with JAMES DOUGHERTY written on it in a jagged script.

I put on disposable gloves before opening the envelope. There's no sense in taking risks. Inside was a dirty little black-and-white zine, self-published and titled *THE FETCH.*

It was sick shit, a disturbing revenge fantasy that could only have come from a disordered mind. The pages were smudged from a cheap photocopier, full of photos of dead dogs and page after page of dense single-spaced rants. The actual plot wasn't that hard to follow, once I picked up the voice of the writer. It was a straightforward story in which a woman's husband is killed by his doppelgänger, sending her on a quest for revenge.

I was rereading it for the second time when I heard the harsh crash of breaking glass. I bolted downstairs where Juana had grabbed a broom and was pointing at glass on the floor from one of the broken picture windows. "I don't know who did it," she yelled. "A kid or someone? They threw a rock. Call the police, Mister James!"

I did. I looked out in the yard and it was empty, all the way to the short fence backing into the scrub of the canyon.

I went upstairs then, racing up them two at a time. My bedroom door was still closed. I threw it open, unsure what I'd find.

Marcia was half-asleep, stirring lightly, still wearing the same pajamas she'd gone to bed in. My presence woke her all the way. She murmured right as I heard the sound of the sirens.

I walked in and closed the door, shutting out the sounds of arriving police, and laid down by her side, putting an arm gently on her back. She blinked and sat up, her hair a mess, her eyes sleepy-lidded.

Everything was like it was before. Except for the bag of *Mahalo Brand Macadamia* nuts left on the bedside.

It's been a few weeks since then. I've bought a gun. I keep the outside doors locked and installed some floodlights. I told Juana that Marcia had a drinking problem and that, if she ever finds her waiting outside in the morning, she shouldn't let her in without telling me first.

I don't live in fear. I don't let myself. It's easy if you want. You just don't let yourself think about it. Don't let yourself see.

And I stay busy; that's the other key. My top priority these days is enjoying my well-deserved success, and that means working on me. Making myself a priority. I've gained so much and I don't want to lose any of it.

Not writing doesn't take up very much time. I keep a full schedule of yoga, transcendental meditation, Zen, AA, CBT, Jungian analysis, equine therapy, encounter therapy, and primal scream; all of it intended to get to the roots of my self-destructive impulses and help with a little of the old self-esteem.

I really like the Zen stuff. I even had one of the koans—the pithy paradoxical phrases meant to snap your brain into enlightenment— made into a poster: "If you meet the Buddha on the road…Kill him!" It's good advice.

That's what I keep coming back to—the thing I keep circling around. They say that hell is the gulf between who you could have been and who you ended up as. But for me? I've learned to reject that kind of binary thinking, that all-or-nothing striving. Success isn't a destination, it's a journey. Any minute spent worrying about "what might have been" is another minute that comes between you and "what still could be."

All the efforts have been working so far, they really have. I've avoided whatever impostor syndrome so plagued JD, the one that led him to an early grave. Taking care of that one is easy at least. I know I'm no impostor. It's the one thing I'm truly certain of: no one else is responsible for my success in life but me.

The truth—the most essential truth of all—is that this was all meant to be. It's all a matter of asking the universe for what you want and then letting it give it to you.

There are times I do feel guilt about some things. The other Marcia. She didn't deserve any of it; she was just caught up in things beyond her understanding. But hell, that's life isn't it?

When it comes to JD, I feel just fine. I don't regret doing what I did to him, what I had to do. You can call me a murderer. I'd just say I embarked on a journey of radical self-improvement.

Sometimes, in the grey and pallid light of another sleepless 4:00 am, I think it should be harder. I wonder if I should feel guilty over the way things went down with JD. But those moments pass. I just have to remember that killing my best self was easy. I'd already had a lifetime's worth of practice.